CIRCUS DAY

A Novel of Suspense

Caroline Crane

Dodd, Mead & Company
New York

Published by Dodd, Mead & Company, Inc.
79 Madison Avenue, New York, N.Y. 10016
Distributed in Canada by
McClelland and Stewart Limited, Toronto
Manufactured in the United States of America
Designed by Erich Hobbing

First Edition

LIBRARY OF CONGRESS CATALOGING-IN-PUBLICATION DATA

Crane, Caroline.
  Circus day.

  I. Title.
PS3553.R2695C5   1986   813'.54   85-27393
ISBN 0-396-08774-4

For Jack, Johanna,
Chris, and Mike

With happy memories
of Blue Sky and my Leopard

CIRCUS DAY

Chapter One

"That's marvelous," Kate Armstrong said to the man in the dry-cleaning shop. "I really appreciate it. Thank you."

He eyed her with suspicion. Probably he thought she was being sarcastic about the ten minutes it had taken him to find the suit.

"I mean it," she explained, as four-year-old Darren tugged at her hand. "My husband's going away on a trip, and there would have been murder if I hadn't gotten his suit. He has his heart set on this suit."

Darren tugged again.

"Just a minute, honey." She removed her hand from his grasp and took out her wallet.

As they left the store, Darren said, "You talk too much. You tell everybody everything."

Kate blinked in surprise and tried not to feel hurt. But words like that, coming from her own little boy, seemed a betrayal.

Of course they were really his father's words. Ted would say a thing like that when he was exasperated, and the children picked it up. By now, the whole family saw her as a harebrained blabbermouth.

"I think it's nice to talk to people," she said. "It's a friendly thing to do."

Carefully she laid the suit on top of her groceries and closed the back of the station wagon. She opened both front windows to let in the warm May air. In the distance, a siren screamed.

Darren bounced in his seat. "A fire!"

"You wouldn't think it was such fun if it were our house," she said.

"I want to see the fire engine."

"No, we'd only get in the way. And the ice cream would melt, and Candy would come home and find the house locked—"

She was doing it again. All she had needed to say was no.

"Mommy, look!"

They were crossing Elton Avenue. She glanced briefly at where he was pointing and saw chaos. Flashing red lights. At least two police cars. She didn't think it was a fire.

"What are they doing?" he asked.

"I can't imagine. Maybe it will be on the radio."

He reached for the knob.

"Not this radio, Darren, the one at home. This one doesn't get local news."

He bounced again, impatiently.

"Maybe it will be in the newspaper," she said.

It was after three o'clock. She watched for Candy walking home with her girlfriends. She still felt terrified at the thought of Candy on her own, even in a group, and even with crossing guards at the main intersections. For several months of that first-grade year, Kate had driven her to and from school every day. Candy had protested, saying she wanted to walk with her friends. Kate had taken to transporting the friends, too, until their mothers talked her out of it.

"Children have to learn independence," the mothers said. "They have to know that we trust them."

2

Probably they felt guilty because they didn't want to help with the transportation.

Finally she saw Candy just turning in at Oyster Drive. Candy waved, then shook her head at the offer of a ride. She was three houses from home.

"There's Daddy's car," said Darren.

"Where?"

"Back there."

She looked in the rear-view mirror. She saw Ted's car stop when it reached Candy and saw Candy run to climb in.

"He's early," said Kate. "He must be in a hurry to get going on that trip."

They converged at the house. Each of the children carried in a bag of groceries, and Ted carried his suit.

"How come you're home so early?" she asked. "I thought the plane didn't leave until seven."

"It takes a while to get to the airport," Ted replied. "Thanks for bringing my suit."

"Any time." She reached up and kissed his cheek.

Darren capered ecstatically. "Daddy, we saw police cars!"

"I hope they weren't chasing your mother."

"No, it was something on Elton," said Kate. "I couldn't see what. Probably an accident."

After putting away the groceries, she went upstairs to their bedroom, where Ted was packing his weekend bag. He had turned on the clock radio and was listening to music. Sweet music, for slow dancing, or dreaming.

She picked up a pair of socks and rolled them. "I still don't see why they have to have it on a weekend."

"Those are vicissitudes of life," he said.

"But a weekend? It doesn't give you any time for yourself. Or us."

Apparently she had struck a defensive nerve.

3

"Look, do you think I want to spend my weekend at a dumb seminar, as you call it?"

She was not at all sure that he didn't. He had seemed quite excited about the idea, as he was by nearly everything connected with the progress of his career.

"Are they going to give you some time off to make up for the weekend?"

"I don't know. It's a motivational seminar. I'm supposed to get so motivated I won't want time off." He grinned.

"Who else is going?"

"Me. Elaine Gusman."

"The Elaine I met at your office party?"

"That's the one."

She wished she hadn't asked. Everything except his family seemed to come first with him. Certainly his job did. And this Elaine, whatever her name was.

"How come you're taking so many shirts, if it's only two days?" she asked.

"Because it's business. I want to look my best. In those smoky rooms, you can do a fast wilt."

"Do you mean you're going to go up and change every time there's a break?"

He waved her to be quiet as the sensuous music faded. An excited voice told them about the merchandise to be found at Geary's Lawn Shop.

"I want the traffic report," Ted whispered.

"And now the news," said another voice. "In our top story at this hour, two masked gunmen held up the Ocean Bank of Belle Harbor just before three o'clock this afternoon. A security guard was shot and killed, and a woman bystander seriously wounded. It's unclear at this time just how the gunfire started. The bandits escaped with an undisclosed amount of cash. It was the first holdup in the Ocean Bank's sixty-year history."

"Oh, my God," breathed Kate. Ted, fearing she was

4

going to say more, waved his hand again. She left him and went out to the backyard, where Darren was playing with his trucks.

"I found out what the police cars were all about," she said. "It was on the radio just now. A bank robbery."

Darren's mouth opened, and he sat clutching his steam shovel.

Then he brightened. "Like on television?"

"Well, sort of, I guess."

"Ooo, goody!"

"Not goody, Darren. Some people were hurt."

"Can we go and see it?" he asked.

"No, it's finished now. There's nothing to see."

"Next time can we?"

"Sure. We'll put ourselves on their mailing list."

He returned to his trucks, humming an engine noise as he dug in the sand that had spilled from his sandbox. Inside the kitchen, the telephone rang.

It was Pam Haskell, inviting them all to a barbecue on Saturday evening.

"I know this is last minute," Pam apologized, "but—"

"Ted's not going to be here," said Kate. "He's leaving for Chicago in just a little while."

"How about you? Will you and the kids come over?"

"Oh, okay, if you're sure it's all right."

She had thought they wouldn't want her. In their couple-oriented society, she felt awkward without Ted. But it would be nice for the children.

"If it rains," said Pam, "we'll have it next week, okay?"

That was better. Ted would be home next week. Unless he signed up for another seminar. But they couldn't have them all the time.

She went back upstairs. "You're missing a barbecue tomorrow night," she told him.

"Can't be helped. Would you be a sweetie and get my toothbrush from the bathroom?"

5

He was packing his toiletry kit. The electric shaver. The lotion. The spice-scented antiperspirant. He had bought new toothpaste, a kind that would leave his breath minty fresh. And green mouthwash in a plastic bottle.

"You're not taking any chances, are you?" she asked.

"I told you I want to make a good impression."

"Are you sure this doesn't have anything to do with Elaine?"

"Why should it have anything to do with Elaine? She sees me every day."

"So do your bosses, don't they?"

"What bosses? They won't even be there. I'll be meeting new people."

"Don't tell me you're looking for another job!"

"It never hurts to make new contacts. They might come in handy sometime."

"Ted, can't you think about anything besides your career?"

He stared at her as though she had lost her mind.

"Sure I do, a lot of things. The nuclear arms race—"

"I mean your family."

"What do you think my career is *for*?"

"But it's not *that* important. I'd rather go barefooted and see you now and then, and so would the kids."

"That's ridiculous," he said.

"Maybe, a little. But I think it's just a rationalization, that you're doing it all for us. I think it's really because it's more interesting than we are. I don't blame you for being bored with little kids and their chatter, and a woman whose whole life is nothing but little-kid chatter."

In two steps he was across the room, pulling her down onto the bed, and rumpling his clothes in the process.

"What are you talking about?" he demanded, kissing her forehead and nose.

He always did that. He acted as though the whole problem were one of sexual deprivation. Why couldn't he understand that she only wanted to feel as if she mattered?

She returned his kisses because he was going away. Then she said, "I know I'm not very interesting right now, but as soon as Darren starts first grade, I'm going to look for a job, okay?"

"Doing what?"

"Well, I guess I can find something. I'm able-bodied and mentally competent, even if I didn't finish college."

She hadn't meant to rub it in. It was because of Ted and his own college studies that she hadn't finished. They had married too soon.

"Fine with me, if that's what you want to do." He got up and resumed his packing.

"You really don't mind?"

"Why should I mind, as long as you think you can handle it?"

"You mean, as long as I don't neglect you." *The way you neglect me.*

"Not just myself. I was thinking of the kids. They're pretty small to be on their own."

"I wasn't exactly planning to leave them alone." *And why can't you help take care of them? They're your kids, too.*

"After all," he pointed out, "they are your first responsibility."

"I'm aware of that, Ted. And come to think of it, I'd better give them something to eat before we leave for the airport."

He closed his toiletry case. There was a slight frown between his deep blue eyes.

"You don't have to go to the airport," he said. "I'll drive myself."

"But then you'd have to park, and that's expensive."

7

"This is a business trip, remember? It's on the company."

"I want to go. And the kids would like it, too. They love the airport."

More kisses. "This time it's impractical, okay? If you take me there, then you'll have to meet me because I won't have a car, and I'll be coming in late at night."

"How late?"

"Nine, ten . . ."

She picked at a quilted tulip on the bedspread. All day she had looked forward to their trip to the airport, and the children's excitement, and feeling necessary as she delivered him to his flight. Now they would simply watch him drive away, and instead of necessary, she would feel left out.

"What's wrong?" he asked.

"Nothing. It's just that I really wanted to go. I'm a little disappointed."

He stood with his arms folded and nodded understandingly.

"Next time, okay? Thanks for being a sport about it." A pat under the chin. "I've got to get moving."

"You are. You're all packed."

"Have to shave. Take a shower."

"Do the meetings start tonight?"

"No, but I'll be seeing people when I get there."

"Oh—right. Well, have a nice shower."

After he had locked himself in the bathroom, she wrapped two of her chocolate-chip cookies, along with a note that said "I love you," and hid them in his suitcase. She put them next to his pajamas, so he would find them that night, and then she went back to the kitchen.

Candy grabbed her around the waist. "When are we going to the airport?"

8

"We're not," said Kate. "I'm really sorry, kids, but Daddy has other plans. He's driving himself."

Darren wailed, "But I want to go!"

"Mommy?" Candy jittered with excitement. "Can we go to the mall tomorrow? They told us at school there's going to be a circus day, with clowns and things."

At six years old, Candy's face was still round with baby softness, but her eyes were dark and flashing. They were her mother's eyes, except that Kate's did not flash.

"I want to go," Candy emphasized.

"We'll see."

"I want to go to the beach," said Darren.

"It's too cold for the beach," Candy argued. "Mommy?"

"I said we'll see. Maybe we can do both. We can go to the mall in the morning—"

"Circus Day starts at twelve."

They couldn't do both. Circus Day would cut right into the middle of it, and the beach would be too chilly in the morning.

In half an hour Ted was ready, shaven, dressed, his damp hair neatly combed to accentuate its natural wave. It was that wave and the intense blue eyes that had first attracted her when they met in college. She had soon found other, less superficial attributes but had never gotten over his good looks.

"I'm off," he said, kissing the children first and saving a special embrace for her. The children danced around him. Deftly he peeled them away so they wouldn't get his clothes mussed or dirty.

They followed him out to the car. Kate noticed that the sunshine had gone and the sky had clouded over. A beautiful May day had simply vanished.

"Good-bye, Daddy!"

"Good-bye, kids." He backed out of the driveway, smiled, waved, and was gone.

Darren's face puckered. "I want to go to the airport."

"Some other time," said Kate. She herded them into the house and parked them in front of the television set while she cooked their hamburger supper.

The house seemed lonely without Ted. She turned on the radio for company.

It made her think of the music he had been listening to. That was a local station and he had wanted the local traffic, but she wondered if there was some other reason, too. Some daydreamy, glowy-eyed reason. Sweet music wasn't usually his choice.

It was the traffic report, she told herself.

They were giving it now. Westbound traffic was running smoothly. He would have no trouble getting to the airport on time. It was the eastbound traffic, out to the Island from New York City, that was heavy.

There was more music, and then the news.

"Police are still searching for two gunmen involved in a shoot-out at a Belle Harbor bank this afternoon. A black sedan, which has been tentatively identified as the getaway car, was found abandoned near the railroad tracks a mile from the Ocean Bank. The car had earlier been reported stolen. Police theorize that the bandits may have hopped a New York–bound train. Both men were described as between five feet ten and six feet; one heavyset, wearing dark pants and a tan jacket, the other in jeans with a short black jacket or shirt. The men are said to be armed and dangerous. A Belle Harbor housewife, injured in the holdup, is listed in critical condition at the Meadowbrook Hospital. We'll have the weather report after this message."

Candy wandered out to the kitchen in time to hear a prediction of rain for Saturday.

"Oh, goody, then we can't go to the beach, can we, Mommy? Dar-ren!" She ran back to the living room, and

Kate heard their voices, first in argument and then happily conferring.

She dreaded the mall on a rainy Saturday, crowded with small children, and strollers coming at her legs like an armored assault.

On the other hand, it would be fun for Candy and Darren. And because of that, she would enjoy it, too.

Chapter Two

Ted switched on the car radio and listened to music. He was on his way, and he felt purposeful. The weekend promised to be an adventure of sorts. He was curious about these seminars.

Besides, it would be a change from cutting the grass. He should have reminded Kate about that grass.

He drove through Saltport, the town that adjoined Belle Harbor, past the gates that led to the sprawling Hyland Aircraft plant where he worked, along a wide street of shopping malls and fast-food places, to an apartment house on Royal Street.

It was not an elegant building. There was something poignant about the way Elaine Gusman lived, the sole support of a demanding, arthritic mother and mainstay of a divorced younger sister with three kids. Not much left for herself, and yet she was cheerful about it. He gave the doorbell three short rings, then went back to his car and waited.

In a little more than a minute, she arrived. She had changed from her business suit to a softer gray one with a long, loose jacket, and a white scarf trailing at her neck. As he took her bag and set it in the trunk, he smelled her perfume. She never wore perfume at the office.

He opened the door for her, and she slid gracefully into

the front seat. Even though it was a low car and she was tall, she managed it with extraordinary grace.

"I'm telling you, that new program," she said. "I thought I wasn't going to get away at all. Especially because I think that little snip Keith is after my job. Hell, let's make a promise to each other, okay? No shoptalk this weekend."

"But it's a working weekend," he pointed out.

"Okay, so we'll work when we work, and the rest of the time we'll have fun. It *is* going to be fun."

"We'll hope so."

"I love going on trips, don't you?"

"Pretty much."

"Only pretty much? Oh, of course, your family." Her fingers brushed his knee. "But don't you like those luxurious hotels and feeling like a VIP?"

"That part I like," he agreed, thinking that he rarely felt special at home. They were usually too busy to bother with him.

It was true that they had all come out to see him off. But that had been part of the trip.

She moved as close to him as she could in the bucket seat. He had never traveled with Elaine before. Was this going to be a problem? He drove back out to Castle Avenue and headed for the parkway.

"It got cloudy," she said.

"It's supposed to rain tomorrow."

"Naturally. It's a weekend. How are the kids?"

She had asked him that this morning. He was flattered by her interest.

"They're okay. Full of energy. I don't know where they get it."

"And Kate?"

"She's okay, too. Just a little put out that they couldn't all escort me to the airport."

"Oh, well, then she'd have had to drive back alone."

13

"She's done it before, but I thought this was easier. If I have the car with me, then there's no hassle in case I decide to change my return flight." And maybe it had something to do with the fact of Elaine's presence and not wanting Kate to worry about it and give him a hard time later, thinking that his devotion to his job had anything to do with people like Elaine.

They arrived at the airport early and went to the lounge reserved for frequent travelers. He ordered drinks, and they sat together on a sofa for two, with a small table in front of them.

Elaine nibbled on peanuts from a glass bowl.

"This is one of the things I like," she said. "I like the way they pamper you in these places. And you can drink all you want without worrying that you have to drive home."

"Very true. I never thought of that aspect."

He liked the relaxed way she sat, with her long legs crossed at the ankle, her long, blond hair in a shining knot at the back of her head. Her long fingers wrapped around her glass.

When she gave him a cozy smile, he realized that he had been staring at her. Flustered, he stirred the ice in his own drink and decided to call Kate.

"What happened?" she asked when she heard his voice. "Did you get stuck somewhere?"

"No, I'm at the airport. Just thought I'd touch base and see how things are going."

"We're watching television," she said.

"Sounds exciting."

"Terribly."

"What are you doing tomorrow?"

"I guess we're going to Circus Day. There doesn't seem any way out. And then the barbecue, if it doesn't rain."

"The radio says rain," he told her. "But it could stop. Give my love to the kids."

"I will. Have a great seminar."

He was sure he would have a great seminar. Even if it wasn't actually great, it ought to be stimulating. Forward-moving. That was what he liked.

Hell, he had forgotten to tell her about the grass. She would have to wait till Sunday anyway, if it was going to rain tomorrow. He'd remind her the next time he called.

Kate kept the radio on. Long after the dishes were washed and the counters wiped, she stayed in the kitchen, listening.

The plane had not yet taken off. It would only be an hour's flight, but she had a terrible feeling, a sense of foreboding. Something would happen that weekend. She wasn't sure what, or how, or when.

She had never been psychic. Probably she only worried because Ted was away. If she thought something bad would happen, then it wouldn't. Disasters rarely came when they were expected.

On the radio, they talked about the bank robbery. About the rain tomorrow, heavy at times. She hated driving in the rain, especially heavy rain, but she couldn't deprive them of Circus Day. That sort of thing was part of being a parent. One assumed more responsibilities than she had ever imagined when one undertook to have children.

In spite of the clouds, the evening was long and light, and Darren, as usual, fought going to bed.

"Why do I have to go first?"

"Because you're younger and you need more sleep. Candy's going to bed right after you."

For once, Candy followed without an argument. She was on her good behavior, thanks to Circus Day.

When both children were in bed, if not asleep, Kate turned on the television. If there were a major air disaster, they would interrupt the program with a bulletin.

15

She selected a movie that kept her amused until the eleven o'clock news.

She hoped Ted would call to assure her that he had arrived safely. But he had called once, and probably that was it for the night. He was already in Chicago, no doubt wearing a clean shirt and having a drink with some of those influential contacts he expected to make. All she had to get through now was his return flight. And then the next trip, and the next, and the next . . .

Elaine's hands were on his arm in the hotel's cocktail lounge. She had long, rosy pink fingernails, beautifully shaped.

"We could go up to my place," she said.

"Your place?" With that mother of hers?

"My room, silly. I have this crazy idea that I want some champagne, and it's ridiculous if you order it by the glass."

"We could get a bottle here."

"Oh, come on. Let's relax."

It sounded good, as long as he could keep them both under control. He was fairly sure she was past the point of that herself.

He stood up. He, too, had drunk quite a bit, but he wasn't dizzy. It was just as well. He didn't need a hangover tomorrow, with those seminars.

Elaine's room was on the same floor as his, around a corner and down another hallway. As soon as they entered, she slipped out of her shoes.

"I just hate shoes, don't you?"

"I really don't think much about it," he had to admit.

"Well, take yours off anyway. I don't even like to look at them."

He did as he was told, while she called room service to order a bottle of champagne and some food to go with it.

The ordering took a while, because they didn't have quiche, which she wanted, and she was not in the mood for crackers and cheese. Finally she settled on cheesecake.

"It's a weird combination," she apologized to him.

"I think it's perfect."

"Do you really?"

After room service had come and gone, she double-locked the door and put on the chain. She set their tray on a small table next to the window, which was discreetly concealed by drawn drapes.

He poured the champagne, and they touched glasses. Elaine stretched out her legs, sighing happily.

"This is the life. It sure beats a weekend at home, listening to Mom."

Poor girl, he thought, watching her. She probably did have it rather dreary.

But then, whose life was undiluted excitement?

A person could make it exciting, as she was doing now with her perfume and champagne, and moving her chair closer to his. They were big, round chairs, like the seats in his car, but again she seemed adept at closing the distance.

He twitched nervously and looked down at the toes wiggling inside his dark gray socks.

"Maybe I ought to call," he said.

"Call what?"

"My wife. She worries whenever I go anywhere."

"She worries?" Elaine's eyes grew large and swimmingly green.

"About the flight. She wants to know when I'm back on the ground. In one piece."

"That's silly. If anything happened, she'd hear about it. And she could collect all the lovely insurance. Don't you think maybe she worries a little too much?"

"What do you mean?"

"I'm not saying it's true in her case, but sometimes when a person worries—oh, never mind."

"Do you mean she might have an unconscious wish for something to happen?"

Elaine said nothing. He was sure she must be wrong. Kate was nuts about him.

"Or"—she crossed her legs and ran a hand lightly along the side of her thigh—"maybe she's just very dependent."

He liked that better. "It could well be. I'm the breadwinner and the faucet-fixer. It must bother her to think of facing life on her own."

"Has she ever worked?"

"Of course. She quit college and worked while I went to school. Thought she could go back later, but by the time I got my Master's, we were having Candy."

"You had candy?"

"My daughter, Candace."

"Oh, right! How could I forget?"

"I'd be surprised if you remembered."

"But they're your kids. That's very important. Well, if you think you should call her, be my guest."

"No, it's silly. She'll have to get over being a nervous wreck. I do travel quite a lot."

Besides, he was perfectly comfortable right where he was. It seemed an unnecessary effort to get up and walk over to the telephone.

Much too comfortable. He shouldn't have had the champagne on top of those other drinks.

And Elaine, as sloshed as he, was nuzzling his arm in a most provocative way.

Sometime during the night, he woke. He thought he was at home, until he smelled her perfume.

She lay curled beside him, wearing only her slip. He

18

eased himself to the edge of the bed and leaned over, trying to reach his watch next to the champagne bucket on the table.

She stirred and mumbled, "Where are you going?"

"I have to get back to my room."

"Aw, stay here. What are you going to do, walk down the hall in your skivvies?"

She was right. He found he was wearing his shorts and shirt, but no trousers. He didn't know what had happened. Maybe he had taken them off to keep them from getting rumpled. Or she had. Or—

He didn't want to think about it. He couldn't remember. Shouldn't have drunk so much. Blacked out like that. He'd feel like hell in the morning. It wasn't what he had come here to do.

And he hadn't even called home, but it was too late now. Too late at night.

Tomorrow was soon enough. Tomorrow, after the meetings. Tell her all about them.

And remind her to cut the grass.

Chapter Three

In Kate's dream, the telephone rang. She answered it and heard Ted's voice. The words he spoke were unintelligible, but she understood their meaning. He loved her and was coming home.

Several times during the night she woke and listened. The house was silent. If he really had called, he would have kept ringing, knowing she was there.

He'll call in the morning, she thought, and fell asleep again.

Finally she opened her eyes to see the room still gloomy and the children standing next to her bed. Candy hugged the immense lavender rabbit her grandmother had given her at Easter. Darren was wrapped in his yellow blanket.

"Uh," said Kate.

"Mommy, it's time to get up," Candy told her.

"Not yet. It's still dark."

"My clock said seven a little while ago."

It had been Ted's idea to give their first-grader a digital clock that displayed the time in large red numerals.

"Sev'n?" The clock radio confirmed it. A look at the window explained the darkness. Heavy clouds. Deep gloom.

She started to ask if Daddy had called, and remembered it was only six-ten in Chicago.

"Can we go to the mall?" asked Candy.

"Is that why you woke me? You said it doesn't start until twelve."

"We didn't wake you."

"I wake up when people stand over my bed and stare at me." Kate rose to her elbow. She hadn't slept well, what with all those telephone dreams. Another few hours would have done it, but that was not to be.

"I can't wait till you folks are in high school," she said, remembering her own late mornings in the teen years. And her mother's nagging. Was there nothing that satisfied parents?

She gave them their breakfast and looked out at the weather. The clouds were very low and gray and the air was warmly humid. She was glad he wasn't flying today. The airport might even be fogged in. She turned on the radio.

More music. It was sprightly this time. Wake-up music. When it faded, she was dismayed to hear an announcement for Circus Day at the Brookside Mall.

"It's going to be mobbed," she groaned.

Candy cheered and clapped her hands. Circus Day was famous.

"Can we go early?" she begged.

"Not too early," said Kate. "First, the mall doesn't open till ten, and second, I want to wait and see if Daddy calls." She wondered what time he started his meetings.

In the middle of the morning, the rain began. All of Long Island became enveloped in a warm, sticky fog.

"Can we still go?" asked Candy, and added helpfully, "The mall's indoors."

"I know it is. I'm waiting to hear from Daddy."

"When can we go?"

"After lunch. We'll have an early lunch. If you're bored, you can straighten your room."

The telephone remained silent. He couldn't have forgotten. He knew how she worried. Something terrible must have happened.

But wouldn't they let her know?

He didn't care. He was there with Elaine, having an exciting time in the real world, doing important things. Home seemed dull to him, and his wife was stupid and uninteresting.

"Mommy, is it lunchtime yet?"

"If you keep bugging me like this," said Kate, sitting at the kitchen table with a cup of coffee, "I'm going to be sick of the mall before we even get there, and I might decide—"

The telephone rang.

"I'll get it!" Candy leaped for the wall phone. "Hello? Oh, hi, Grandma. No, this is Candy. Grandma, did you get the picture I sent you? I drew it myself. They're violets. Do you want to talk to Mommy?"

Kate took the phone. "Hi, Mom."

"You don't sound very enthusiastic," said her mother.

"I'm terribly enthusiastic. I just thought it might be Ted. He hasn't called."

"No news is good news, most of the time."

"When are you coming out to see us?"

"I was going to suggest you bring the children into town. We could go to a museum."

"Darren's a little young—"

"He's not too young for dinosaurs. You used to love the dinosaurs."

Kate had forgotten about that museum. She had been thinking of art.

"We're all set for today. I promised the kids. Why don't we see what it's like tomorrow? If it's really gorgeous, Darren wanted to go to the beach. You could come with us. I'll give you a call in the morning, okay?"

"Fine," said her mother.

Half an hour later, Candy announced that it was time for lunch. "I even cleaned my room. Sort of."

Kate sighed. There was not much else to do. She took bread and cheese from the refrigerator and heated the broiler for grilled sandwiches.

"We're not going right at twelve, you understand," she told the children. "I want to see if Daddy calls during his lunch break. That should be about one."

"We're never going to get to the mall," Candy wailed.

"Of course we are. Don't be so silly."

At one-forty, there had still been no word from Ted. She thought of calling his hotel and leaving a message. It would only alarm him. He would say, "What did you have to waste all that money for?" and she would feel silly.

"It's after lunch," Candy reminded her.

Kate looked out at the pouring, pelting rain. "I was hoping it would let up."

"Mommy, Circus Day will be all over before we get there!"

"I'll take my umbrella," offered Darren.

She couldn't put it off any longer, and the rain showed no sign of letting up.

Since the day was warm and muggy, she dressed them in lightweight jackets and carried Ted's umbrella, which was four times the size of Darren's. She wondered if it was raining in Chicago.

As soon as the car was out of the garage, its windows began to fog. Heavy rain blurred the windshield in spite of the wipers. Dashing back to lock the garage, she could see the reason for automatic doors. It was something they couldn't afford—all because she had no job.

23

"Okay, here goes." She backed her long station wagon down the driveway. "Watch for traffic. I can't see a thing."

"Me either," said Darren. "The window's all mushy."

"There's nothing coming," Candy announced.

Everybody else had enough sense to stay home. Kate hoped it meant the mall would not be packed. She proceeded out to the street and drove slowly, with the wipers turned to high speed.

The mall was in Saltport, just over the Belle Harbor line. In spite of the weather and her hopes, the parking lot seemed full. After circling it once, she found a spot at the far end of a row. They all crowded under one umbrella and hurried to the nearest entrance, soaking their shoes.

Once inside, they could forget the gloomy weather. The entire mall was brightly decorated with lights, streamers, and clusters of balloons. Loudspeakers blared tinkling circus music while clowns paraded back and forth, passing out more balloons. Outside the health-food store, a trained seal played "America" on a set of horns.

"Stay close to me," Kate told the children. "You could get lost in this madness. Darren, hold my hand."

"Where's the elfants?" he asked. "Candy said there's going to be elfants."

Candy giggled. Kate replied, "I shouldn't think so. That would be dangerous, with so many people." She nudged Candy. "Shame on you."

They stopped to watch a clown perform magic tricks with scarves, cards, and mirrors. His hair was a mop of red yarn, his costume green and white stripes, and he wore a bow tie with two tiny lightbulbs that winked on and off.

Candy gaped at the young blond girl who accompanied him, pushing a shopping cart filled with the materials for his act.

"Why can't I do that?" she asked. "I never have any fun."

"She's probably his daughter," said Kate. "And you're right, it's real tough having a daddy who can't do tricks."

"I want him to be a magician. All he does is go to Chicago. It's not fair."

The clown smiled at her. "How about a hat? Do you want me to make you a hat?"

Consoled by his attention, Candy stood still while he twisted sheets of bright pink tissue paper into a brimmed cloche with a giant rosette on one side. When it was finished, he gave her a hand mirror so she could see herself. She rewarded him with a gap-toothed smile.

"That's rather nice," said Kate. "For a paper hat, it's quite stylish."

"Would you like one, too?" asked the clown.

"I don't think so. But it is nice."

They walked on to what Darren called the "penny pool." On its shallow, rocky bottom gleamed hundreds of coins that people tossed in with the hope of bringing themselves luck. At the edge of the pool, a group of teenaged boys performed comedy skits and juggling acts.

While the children watched, Kate felt a tightness grip her head: an iron band, a tangle of nerves.

Because of him, she thought.

It wasn't the heavy, damp weather, it was Ted. He was too engrossed in all that fun stuff, or possibly in Elaine. That was why he hadn't called.

He could have spared two minutes.

A pounding began in her forehead above her right eye as they made their way to the end of the mall and turned back, past clowns who handed out food samples, and other clowns who twisted balloons into animal shapes.

"Kids," she said, "I have to get some aspirin."

"Can we have something to eat?" asked Candy.

"I don't think we can get near any food stores, and my aspirin takes priority."

She would never make it. The discount pharmacy was down at the other end. The mall seemed to stretch into infinity and was filled with an impenetrable crowd. The supermarket was mobbed. Impossible to find one's way through all those people to look for a bottle of aspirin. She remembered a smaller drugstore not far away and pushed toward it.

It was barely a slit in the wall. Behind the counter stood a dumpy little man with a gray mustache and a gray cotton jacket. Kate picked out a small container of aspirin.

"Do you know where I could find a drinking fountain?" she asked.

"You don't want to take aspirin at a drinking fountain," said the man. "You could choke on it. Here, wait a second." He disappeared through a narrow door and came back with a paper cup of water.

"Oh, thank you." She opened the aspirin bottle.

"Four!" he exclaimed.

"It's a bad one."

"Now what could be giving you a bad headache today when everybody's having so much fun?"

"Maybe that's why." She swallowed the aspirin two at a time.

"It's because my daddy went to Chicago and he didn't call home," Candy volunteered. "She thinks his airplane crashed."

Kate swayed dizzily. How could Candy know what had been going unspoken through her mind?

But it was no longer the airplane, it was the whole thing. The absorption with work and with the big, exciting world out there. And the people. Elaine.

"I wouldn't worry," said the druggist. "If anything happened to that plane, you'd know it."

"Well, it isn't just that," Kate began.

"Ah."

He understood.

They all understood more than she expected. Maybe because, as usual, she talked too much.

"Can't have you feeling bad," he said. "This is supposed to be a happy day." He rummaged under the counter.

"It's really all right."

"Maybe this will help." He handed her a sample vial of perfume. *Châle Indien*, it said on the label.

"Oh, thank you, but you really don't have to."

"It's no problem."

It probably wasn't. He had undoubtedly gotten it free.

"And now for the kiddies." From a rack on the counter he took two gaily feathered key rings, a bright pink one for Candy and a yellow one for Darren.

"Why, that's perfect. It matches your coat and hat," Kate exclaimed. "And the yellow one goes with Darren's blanket. It's very nice of you, sir." Her headache had not improved, but already she felt better. If only Ted could be as thoughtful, as sensitive.

They went back out to the mall, bought ice-cream cones at Baskin-Robbins, and watched the redheaded clown give another magic show.

"Have we seen enough?" She sensed that Darren was tired, and she wanted to get home. There was still a chance that Ted might call when the meetings ended that afternoon.

Candy muttered a regretful "I guess so." She turned for a last look at the clown and his enviable daughter. The blond girl smiled at her. Candy smiled back. Kate took her hand, and they went out through the nearby exit, which was closest to their car.

They stood under a marquee, assessing the rain, while she disentangled the umbrella from her purse handle. She was only vaguely aware of a man standing next to her, another refugee from the weather.

"I don't want my hat to get wet," said Candy.

"Then you'd better put it inside your jacket."

The man commented, "That's a pretty hat."

Kate glanced at him. He was young, and not bad looking, from what she could see. His eyes were a clear blue, lighter than Ted's. His coat collar was turned up, covering the lower part of his face. A lock of dark blond hair trailed down his forehead from under a black knitted cap.

"Some lousy weather," he said. "Are you here by yourself?"

"Well, with my children." She held the umbrella away from them and pressed the button that made it open.

"You had to drive here by yourself in the rain? What happened, your husband couldn't bring you?"

"He's in Chicago. And I consider myself a perfectly competent driver."

"Glad to hear that. Where's your car?"

"It's over—"

Too late, she realized that he had no business asking.

It was too late now to say that she was waiting for someone to pick her up. And she had given away the car's location by raising her face when she started to speak.

He nudged them forward. "Let's get moving."

The children stared. It was a real gun. They had never seen a real one before.

Run, she wanted to tell them. *Run inside.*

It was too late.

She looked back toward the door, but no one was there to help them.

Chapter Four

Gesturing with his gun, he edged them away from the marquee. They stepped out into the rain.

She forgot to raise her umbrella until the heavy drops splashed on her head and face. The children huddled close to her.

Ted, help me. Ted. Please.

Ted was in Chicago. Someone. Anyone. In all that distance, someone would have to come along.

"Where's your car?" he repeated, close to her ear.

She turned, trying to think of something, and again saw the gun.

Someone. Please. Come.

She could not believe that there was no one around.

Near the deserted garden shop, a figure moved through the rain.

Oh, God. Thank you, God.

The figure walked toward them. It was a large, burly man in a tan jacket.

Again close to her ear: "Is this your car?"

She looked up at the second man. A heavy, impassive face. Raindrops running down his head, through his dark, wiry hair.

She had stopped next to her car. Led them right to it.

This couldn't be happening. They hadn't given her a chance.

"Open up, lady."

The keys. Her jacket pocket.

No, in her purse. Juggling the umbrella, she opened her purse and took out the keys.

It wouldn't fit. It was the trunk key with the round head.

"Get with it, lady. It's wet out here."

The other. The square one. She fumbled at the door lock.

It opened. The second man reached in to unlock the back door, then herded the children inside. He pushed them over and climbed in beside them.

In his left hand was a gun, pointed at her children.

The first man slid across the front seat to the passenger side and motioned her into the car.

She folded her umbrella. Shook the rain off it. There was rain everywhere. It streamed down her face.

She got in under the wheel. Her own car. Her familiar car.

Her teeth chattered. She sat studying the dashboard. "I can't," she said.

"You told me you're a good driver. Get it going."

"I—I was bragging. I really—I'm still learning. My husband—"

"Get it going, lady. We don't have time."

The engine sputtered, then stopped. Again and again she turned the key. She smelled gas, knew she had flooded it, but she had to be doing something.

"It's the rain," she said. "It won't start."

The burly man leaned forward. "Hold the pedal down."

Hold it down. Yes, that was right. She pressed the gas pedal to the floor and turned the key again. On the second try, it caught.

She had done it.

"Let's get out of here," said the man beside her.

She put the car into gear and started to back. The brake warning light glowed red. She released the hand brake and turned on the wipers. Thank God. Her mind was clearer now. She had done something right.

She drove to the parking lot exit and had to stop for a traffic light.

"Which way?" she asked.

"That way." He pointed to the right. "Go for the parkway."

"Which—which parkway?"

"Don't be cute, understand?"

She hadn't meant to be cute. There were so many choices. She supposed they wanted the nearest one. Whatever it took to get away, off the Island.

They're going to kill us. But first they have to take us someplace where nobody will hear the shots.

In the mirror she could see Darren's face, tense with fear. Little Darren, only four years old.

How could she have done it? A harebrained blabbermouth. She couldn't have known, but if only she hadn't talked. There was no reason to tell him anything.

They were driving through Saltport. Ted took this way to work. But Ted was in Chicago.

"What do I do," she asked faintly, "when we get to the parkway? Do you want to go east or west?"

He didn't answer. Probably west, toward the mainland, but she had to know.

"At the parkway," she said again, more loudly, "do you want to go east or west?"

Maybe he didn't know which was which. Maybe he didn't live around here or know the area.

"East goes out to eastern Long Island," she explained, "toward Riverhead and Montauk. West goes to New York City. So which—"

31

"New York."

She would have to drive in the city, in a crush of heavy traffic squeezing past double- and triple-parked trucks, of one-way streets and masses of pedestrians dashing across in the middle of the block. She would have to slam on the brakes. His gun would go off—

But there would be people. People everywhere. She could get mixed up and go the wrong way on a one-way street. She could run a red light.

She could get her children shot by that man in the back seat.

The windshield had fogged over. She tried to wipe away the steam.

"Cut that out."

He thought she was signaling.

"I can't see." She opened her window. The outside air was humid, too.

"Close it."

"But I—"

The defroster. She turned it on. A blast of heat came through the vents. She reached for the lever to adjust it.

Something green loomed outside and was gone. The road sign. For the parkway.

She gave a low moan. "I went past it. I didn't see it."

"What?"

"The ramp. For the parkway. I didn't see it. I—"

She would have to make a U-turn. *I can't.* It was a wide, busy street. Saturday. Everybody was driving along that street.

"I can't turn around. There's no place. I can't!"

A red light. My God, she hadn't seen it. She stopped with a jolt. *Oh, God, oh, God.*

"Watch it, lady."

"I can't *do* this. I'm so—"

The light changed to a green arrow. She turned left

32

into a gas station and came out onto a side road. She was thinking clearly now. Another light, and she was back on the highway.

Only then did it occur to her that she could have gone on to the next parkway entrance, a few miles ahead.

Carefully this time, she watched for the westbound ramp. She made the turns as smoothly as she could so as not to jar the gun. Which one was he pointing at? Darren or Candy?

There was another gun in the front, pointed at her.

He kept it trained on her even as he leaned forward to peer at the radio.

"Does that thing work? Put it on. Get some news."

She turned the knob. The music was swaying, rhythmic. "The Skaters' Waltz."

"News!"

She poked the buttons until she heard a voice: a commercial for canned tuna fish.

"Maybe you'd better find it," she said. "Ten-ten or eight-eighty. They're both all-news stations."

He grumbled and turned from station to station until he caught a mention of Chile. Something in Chile. He listened, cocking his head toward the radio. From Chile they went to London, and then New York City. "And that's the news. Don't forget to stay tuned for an afternoon of—"

"Where the hell's the Saltport station?"

"That's FM. It's not—not on there."

"Shit."

"It's an old car. It doesn't have FM. I'm sorry."

He turned down the volume and twiddled again with the dial but found no news.

"Where are you taking us?" She had to know.

"Just keep driving."

The road went by as though in a dream. The fog, the rain, the new spring greenery. The other cars.

33

She was dead. The children were dead. They wouldn't even be missed until tomorrow night.

She was supposed to call her mother in the morning.

But her mother wouldn't wait for the call or even wonder what had happened. She would go off to the museum by herself. She was independent. Too independent. She would enjoy the day, never guessing . . .

"How much gas you got?"

She looked at the gauge. "About half a tank."

"Keep going."

She wouldn't tell him the car was a guzzler. She tried to plan what she would do when they stopped for gas.

She could put on her headlights.

But many people were driving with their lights on in the fog and rain.

If the high beams were controlled by a foot button, she could blink an SOS. But it was a lever on the steering column. She had always liked that feature. Until now.

Blabbermouth, she thought again. If she had kept her mouth shut—

If she hadn't stopped for the aspirin. Or the ice cream. If the line at Baskin-Robbins hadn't been so long. Or a little longer.

If Ted had called last night, or even this morning, she would not have waited. She would have been in and out of the mall before this could happen.

They would have taken someone else. Her children, Ted's children, would be safe and someone else's would be dead.

Dead, she thought again, feeling the word.

It was his fault, Ted's, for not caring.

"Take that road up there," said the man.

"Which one?"

She was almost upon it, a road that went off from the parkway and disappeared into the woods. She turned abruptly. The car skidded.

"Watch it!"

"I'm sorry."

With her head pounding, she managed to regain control and followed the road over a low rise.

The man cursed when he saw a house.

He's going to kill us. He wants a place to kill us.

"Keep going."

They passed another house. Ahead of them, a narrow lane forked to the left. He told her to take it.

"I think that's a drive—"

"Take it!"

She had to think of something. Now. *Please, God, help me.*

"Pull over."

They were in a grove of small trees. The ground was low and swampy. Beyond the trees was a roof and part of a house.

They'll see us, she thought. *They'll call the police.*

"Leave that engine on." The man opened his door.

She left the engine on. So he could make a quick getaway after he killed them. They would lie there in the rain.

She waited to be ordered from the car. Instead, he tramped off into the woods and vanished from sight.

Looking for a spot. Maybe he hadn't noticed the house. They would hear the shots.

Moments later he was back. Without a word, he got into the car and closed his door. She waited. Waited to be ordered—

"Get moving."

She reached for the door handle.

"Oh, no, you don't." He raised his gun.

She understood. Get the car moving.

She put it into gear. Her head throbbed so badly she could scarcely see.

Darren said in a small voice, "I have to go, too."

The man turned angrily. "You're going to wait."

"Please?" Kate begged. "He's only four years old. And you know how it hurts."

She was amazed at herself for speaking up. But she was angry. Protective. It gave her courage.

The man considered for a moment. Then he said, "Okay, get out of the car. But make it quick. Stay right there where I can see you."

"Can I go behind a tree?"

"That tree, there." The man pointed to a sapling. Darren scrambled from the car.

She worried about Candy. About herself. That would be more complicated. She was glad that Candy remained silent.

Darren hurried back, zipping his jeans.

The man said, "Get out of here." Meaning her. The car.

There was no place to turn. If she tried it, her wheels would stick in the mud. She looked down at his feet to see if they had messed up her carpet. He wore black sneakers with a knot in one lace. They were wet but not muddy.

"I'll have to back up," she said. "I can't see without the window open."

He did not reply. She cranked down the window and felt the cool air on her face. She had not realized how warm it was in the car.

His voice made her jump.

"What's going on?"

"I had to put on the lights. In case somebody comes up behind us."

She began to back. She felt a sick thumping in her chest. Maybe she would have a heart attack. Then what would happen to the children?

At last she was out on the wider road. She assumed he wanted to return to the parkway. He said nothing.

36

The road looked unfamiliar. But they had come this way. What if she couldn't find the parkway entrance?

He turned the radio knobs. "Where's that station?"

"Which one?"

"The news! News!"

"It's ten-ten or eight-eighty. They both—have news."

A sign pointed to Parkway West. For a moment she couldn't remember whether that was the right direction.

He played with the radio, listening to voices, until he found one that gave the news. Then he turned it low again and sat staring out at the road, watching where she drove.

The parkway was a blur of gray pavement and rain. She felt as though she had been driving along it all her life. As though she had never known anything else.

The children were unnaturally quiet. She wished she could do something, say something. Let them know that she loved them.

Maybe a gunshot wouldn't be so bad. It was quick. And who could tell, the world might end tomorrow, anyway.

She remembered when her mother had cancer.

"You've got to fight," her mother had said. "You've got to fight these things. Don't take it lying down." She had fought it and won.

But how could you fight an enemy with a gun? Two guns?

The man said, "Take that road that goes up there, the Cross Island Parkway. Know where it is?"

"Of course I know where it is."

She knew in theory, but not exactly.

"You'll have to help me look for it," she added meekly. "I can't see very well in the rain." And then, "I don't know how long I can keep this up."

It was a stupid thing to say. She had no choice but to keep it up.

37

As they drew closer to New York City, the traffic became heavier. Cars cut in front of her, splashing the windshield. Others blinded her from behind with headlights turned on because of the fog. Her eyes became glazed. She blinked rapidly and shook her head, trying to clear her vision.

In the rearview mirror, she saw Darren slumped against Candy's shoulder, asleep. Candy was staring at the floor. Kate remembered the festive pink hat with its rosette and wondered where it had gone.

She remembered the little druggist who had tried to cheer them up. *Do you know where we are now, little druggist?*

Her headache was lifting. Or perhaps she had been too distracted to think of it.

Cross Island Parkway. At last.

She glanced at the man. She had asked him to help her, and he hadn't.

"This is the Cross Island," she said as she turned onto it. "Where do I go now?"

"I'll tell you when we get there."

"It's not that easy. I have to know before, so I can be in the right lane. I can't cut across all this traffic."

"Shut up and drive."

Suddenly he leaned forward and turned the radio louder.

"—yesterday, died this morning in a Long Island hospital. Police identified the woman as Mrs. Olive Silver of Belle Harbor. The two fugitives involved in the holdup are still at large. In Brooklyn, a grocery—"

He snapped off the radio.

The man in back said, "Leave it on."

"I don't want to hear about Brooklyn."

Why us? Kate wondered. *Of all the people in the world, why us?*

What had the men been doing there, anyway? Why hadn't they hopped a train, the way the police thought? Because the trains and the stations would be watched. They had hidden all night, waiting.

Why us?

"Watch the road!"

She watched. It was her only chance. Do what they wanted and try to keep everybody calm.

She must have been driving for an hour or more. Nightfall should still have been a long way off, but it seemed to be dark already. She looked at the sky and saw that it was blacker than before. A streak of lightning blazed against the clouds.

Almost immediately, the thunder crashed. Darren woke and gave a frightened cry.

The man in back said angrily, "Shut up that noise."

"It's the thunder," Kate explained. "He probably thought it was your gun going off. They're only children, and they don't understand all this. You can't expect them to know what to do."

Talking too much. She must learn to say only what was necessary.

"It's just the thunder, Darren. Go back to sleep."

Darren was sleepless now. He sat with his mouth turned down, eyeing the gun on the big man's lap.

Poor babies. Her poor, darling babies. If only Ted had called.

If only she had been more careful.

They rounded a bend and suddenly, ahead of them, was a sea of red brake lights. The traffic slowed to a crawl. She pumped her own brake as they entered the jam.

The man beside her looked around anxiously. "Get out of this mess, you hear?"

"There's no way out." She tried to hide her own panic.

"It's moving a little, and nobody can see you with the windows all steamy. Besides, the police think you took a train to New York yesterday."

Brilliant. Now they knew that she had identified them.

As suddenly as it had begun, the congestion eased. She was able to pick up speed. The parkway became a tangle of ramps and bridges, and he was telling her to change lanes.

"Where to?" she asked.

"No questions."

They drove down a ramp onto another parkway. She couldn't remember its name. It was enormously wide. About a million lanes. Somewhere on her right there was water. Above her, a sign pointed to LaGuardia Airport.

They were still on Long Island. Still home. But La-Guardia was very near the end of it.

"Go for the Triborough Bridge. That way that says New England."

"New England?"

God help her, she would be driving all night.

Chapter Five

Hoyt Ave., a sign said. She imagined Hoyt Avenue as a quiet street like her own, and all the people on it comfortably at home watching television or eating dinner.

"Look out!"

Again she stopped with a jolt. She had nearly hit the car in front of her.

She had been hurrying simply because she thought he wanted her to. Now it occurred to her that she could buy that much more time just by slowing down.

"Look," she pleaded, "I'm really tired. It's not easy, driving in all this rain."

"Keep going, understand? And do it right."

"I don't think *you* understand. I'm not a machine. I can't—"

Her rage built. She let it out in a breath. She must buy time, not cut it short by provoking them.

The ramp to the bridge was a long one. The truck in front of her bounced and slammed and spattered her windshield with mud.

New England, he had said. Where in New England? Even most of Connecticut seemed very far away.

Or maybe they were heading toward Canada. Would a fugitive be safe there? How did they mean to negotiate the border crossing?

Maybe they didn't know what a border crossing entailed. She would keep her mouth shut this time and not tell them.

The bridge split into two sections, one that went to Manhattan, the other to the Bronx and New England. Soon they would have to pay a toll. She tried to think how she could catch the attention of the toll collector.

The man reached into his pocket and counted out several coins. He handed them to her as they neared the gate.

"Exact change," he said. "Get in that lane there."

An exact-change lane with an automatic gate. She wouldn't pass a toll collector. Too late, as she tossed the money into the basket, she realized that she could have tried to miss it. Then they would have had to stop. Maybe someone would have come to help her.

But probably the man would have made her go on. Either given her more money or told her to crash through the gate.

"Keep going," he said and pointed out the direction. "New England Turnpike."

Wistfully she watched the road to Manhattan turn off to her right. Manhattan, in a way, was home. Her mother lived there. And she could run a traffic light. . . .

The New England Turnpike was limited access. There would be no red lights to disobey. No pedestrians who might see the gun.

He leaned toward her, pressing against her. She stiffened, then realized he was trying to see the gas gauge.

"We'll have to stop soon," she said. "You should have picked a small foreign car that gets fifty miles to a gallon."

He hadn't picked the car, he had picked her. Because she happened to be there. A woman alone with two small children. And a big mouth. She was especially vulnerable because of the children.

Ted, do you see what you've done?

My fault . . . my fault . . .

Huge diesel trucks roared past her. Bewildering clusters of signs above her head pointed to various routes and exits. She had never driven this way before. She did not know what to expect. He had told her to watch for the New England Turnpike, and she tried to follow the signs.

"It would help," she said, "if I knew where we were going."

"I told you. New England."

"But where? I need to get a fix."

"You need a fix?"

"Not that kind. I need to know approximately where and how long."

"You don't have to know that shit. It's up to me."

"What about your friend? Doesn't he get a vote?"

"He does what I tell him."

So that was it. The younger man ran the show. He was probably the sharper one, and he had put his gorilla in back with her children.

"Do you even know where you want to go?" she asked. "Or are you just going?"

"I told you, lady, no questions."

He didn't understand. Talking helped her to stay alert. She had taken four aspirins. The hum of the tires on wet pavement had a hypnotic effect. It altered her consciousness until the whole thing seemed a wild, improbable dream. If she could—

"Do you know where's Vermont?" asked the man.

Not a dream. His voice had pulled her back.

"Of course. It's next to New Hampshire."

"That's where we're going."

"I don't think you'll get to Vermont on the New England Turnpike," she said.

"Don't give me that. It's New England, right?"

43

He really didn't know. For all his bluster and his gun, he did not know where he was going.

She felt almost apologetic.

"Yes, but you see, the turnpike goes up along the coast, and Vermont is inland."

"So? Keep going, like I told you. I know what I'm doing."

Signs pointed to the Whitestone Bridge and the Throgs Neck Bridge. Back to Long Island. She wondered why he had chosen the Triborough instead of one of those. If she could turn that way and pretend it was a mistake—

He would catch her at it. She could do nothing but keep quiet and obey.

Soon the signs were behind them, and so was the way to Long Island.

Then they were in Westchester County. It was the last part of New York State before New England.

"Do you expect me to drive all the way to Vermont tonight?"

"Whatever I tell you." He fingered the gun. *Relishing its power,* she thought.

"We'll need some gas. Very soon."

He leaned over her to look at the gauge.

"It's empty!" He sounded outraged.

"Not quite. We have a few more miles. There ought to be a service area sometime." She could not remember where. Probably not until Connecticut.

They passed a sign announcing a toll. He dug in his pocket and pulled out a dollar.

If only she could signal. She tried to think of something. Anything.

As she slowed the car, he slipped his gun under his knee. She delivered the bill and received a handful of change. The toll collector never looked into the car. A

human being so near that her fingers brushed his, and it
had done her no good.

After they passed the gate, the man drew out his gun,
crossed his legs and relaxed.

"So how do you get to Vermont?" he asked.

"I'd have to look at a map."

"You got any maps?"

"In the glove compartment."

He began to whistle softly. They were almost out of
New York.

After a while they crossed the state line.

"We're in Connecticut," she told him. He did not re-
spond.

She looked in the back mirror. Both children were
asleep. She was glad they could sleep through this. If only
she could wreck the car before they woke.

But they might wake for one terrified instant. One moment of pain. She didn't want them to have even that.
She had wanted so much for them. . . .

In a few days, people would read about her in the
newspaper. They would drool with horrified fascination
and be glad it hadn't happened to them.

It wasn't fair.

The rain, which had tapered to a drizzle, began to fall
in a great, gushing flood. Cascades streamed down the
windshield. She turned the wipers to high speed and
slowed the car.

"Keep going," ordered the man.

"You idiot, I can't even see! Do you want us to have an
accident?"

He drew in a breath. White-hot fury. She didn't care.

"All right, you want an accident, we'll have one." She
stepped on the gas pedal.

The needle on the gauge had gone well into the red

45

danger zone. If they ran out of gas, she would lose her brakes and steering. They would have to abandon the car, if they didn't crash. She drove faster, blindly, into a smear of lights.

"Hey! Up there!" He pointed ahead.

It was a service area. Her chance to wreck the car had gone.

The man, mumbling about how crazy she was, opened her purse, took out her wallet and removed a ten-dollar bill. "Tell them to fill 'er up."

She almost laughed. "Do you think ten is going to do it?"

He looked for more and didn't find it. She had spent it on yesterday's groceries. While the gas was pumped, he turned to the man in back. The big man rummaged through something, probably the money they had stolen, and came up with a twenty-dollar bill.

Please, she thought. *Please have it be marked.*

But of course it wouldn't be. The bank had not expected a robbery. They would not have had any special bills prepared.

She thought they kept track of serial numbers. She didn't know what they did. The money would be long gone, and so would she, before anyone could trace it here.

The attendant noticed nothing. He was only a young man doing his job, probably counting the hours until it was time to go home to a wife and baby.

She drove on with a tankful of gas. The stop had waked the children. Candy asked, "Are we still here?" and began to cry.

Darren said, "I'm hungry."

"You kids shut up," the big man warned.

"They haven't had anything to eat since lunch," said Kate. The ice cream didn't count.

She wished they were back buying cones in Baskin-

46

Robbins. *Please, please give us another chance.*

As a young child, she had thought she could get whatever she wanted by wishing hard enough. When her wishes were not granted, which they rarely were, she assumed it was only for lack of effort. It took a long time before she understood how many things were entirely out of her hands.

Even now she could not accept it. Especially now. She *had* to find some way of getting back to the mall. Of starting over again. She must wish away those hours.

She drove on, listening to the rhythm of the windshield wipers and one of her children softly weeping. She couldn't tell which one.

The raised highway carried them over Stamford. She knew it was Stamford because it said so on the exit signs. She didn't know whether it was afternoon or evening. Only dirty, gray rain.

What were they going to do in Vermont? They probably had friends there. A safe house.

He hadn't known the cost of gasoline. It meant that he didn't drive, or hadn't in years. But how could he not know? Everybody knew.

Probably in prison. A long, long stretch. He was a vicious, recidivist killer.

If he didn't drive, then he would need her until he reached his destination.

Unless the big man drove.

He did. He had told her to hold down the pedal when the engine flooded. Then why hadn't they just taken the car? Why encumber themselves with—

Hostages. That was it. And if they had taken the car, they would have had to shoot her right there in the parking lot to keep her from reporting the theft. They would have thought she'd do that. If they had let her go, she would have honored any promise.

47

They might have taken the children to ensure her silence. It was far better this way. Oh, *much. Oh, thank you, God.*

The man said, "Take that next exit."

Were they already in Vermont?

This road didn't go there. It went to Boston.

Following his instructions, she drove down a ramp and then along a street that was a mixture of houses, garages, and shops. She hadn't noticed the name of the town.

"There." He pointed ahead.

"Where?"

"The Burger King." His foot twitched impatiently. "Go for the drive-in window."

Was he going to feed the children, or only himself? She felt an unreasoning gratitude when he turned and asked them what they wanted.

"A Big Mac," said Darren.

"A Whopper," Kate explained. "That's what he means."

"What about you?"

"Me?" She hadn't thought of eating. She didn't know if she could.

"What do you want?"

"A . . . a Whopper, I guess. And coffee. Regular."

When they reached the window, he leaned across her and gave their order. He would not trust her to speak. What could she possibly say when they held a gun on her children?

They ate in the parking lot. She couldn't finish her Whopper. She gave most of it to Candy, whose anxiety had increased rather than diminished her appetite. Afterward, he let the children go to the rest room one at a time. He warned them not to play tricks. Their mother would die, he said, if they talked to anybody.

It was the first time Darren had been to a public rest room by himself. How would he manage? Would he

48

really not talk? Her hands lay clenched in her lap until he came skittering back to the car.

"Let's get moving," the man said.

She backed out of their slot, pausing to let a young couple cross in back of her. Watched a group of teenagers pile out of their car. So many people around, and no way to reach them.

She could smash into another car. . . .

"I said get moving."

"Where to?"

"Back to the turnpike."

The rain had slowed again to a drizzle, and the coffee had revived her. She drove back the way they had come and finally saw a sign that directed her to the turnpike.

Chapter Six

Ted hung up the telephone. "She's not home."

"Are you sure you called the right number?" asked Elaine. She was stretched out on his bed, waiting for him to open the champagne. He wished he could share her passion for champagne. Or admit to her that he didn't. At the moment, he would have preferred a beer.

He wished he knew how this whole thing had started. He should have been out meeting people.

"Of course I called the right number. I know my own number."

"Sometimes the lines get screwed up. Didn't you ever dial a number, and you know you did it right, but you still get the wrong one?"

"She probably went to stay with her mother." He flexed his hands and picked up the bottle.

"Where does her mother live?"

"Manhattan. Kate doesn't usually stay over, it's not a big apartment, but you never can tell." He pushed at the cork. It popped off and rolled into a corner.

"To us," said Elaine when the drink was poured. "And to Hyland, and the weekend, and your wife and kids."

To us?

She propped up the pillows, and he sat back with her against the headboard.

"Ted, can I ask you a personal question?"

"Haven't we been getting fairly personal?"

"Yes, and that's why I have the nerve to ask. Are you really happy?"

"Am I what?"

"Are you happy with your life?"

"Why, what do you mean? Because of this weekend?" Oh, hell, did she think he was going to leave Kate and marry her? Or conduct a full-fledged affair? Damnation, this was going to be sticky, especially back at the office.

"In general," she said. "I want to know if you're really, really happy. Do you think you've found what you wanted?"

"Well, sure, within the bounds of reality. Naturally I'd like to be a playboy and spend my time racing cars—"

He realized that she was serious. She didn't expect a flippant answer.

He thought of the chocolate-chip cookies he had found in his suitcase when he dressed that morning. At first it had seemed a reproach after the night he had spent with Elaine, but that, of course, was his own guilty conscience speaking. Kate couldn't possibly have known it was going to happen, or even that it did.

"I don't know how to say this," he began.

"Okay, okay, I get the picture. That's all I wanted. It's fine with me. I'll have you know, I wasn't looking for anything serious, either."

"Serious?"

"Oh, you know." She gave him a playful shove, spilling drops of champagne on the bed. "I didn't mean serious, like leaving the wife and kiddies. I wasn't even thinking of anything like that. It wouldn't be my scene, the barbecue-on-the-patio bit."

"Elaine—"

"Forget it. We're just having fun this weekend, aren't we? All work and no play is no good, right?"

51

"That's right, but—"

"And it's our last night, so let's drink up and not talk about it. Ever. Okay?"

"That's fine with me," he said as he refilled her glass.

Kate could not sleep. It was freezing in the car. Back on Long Island it had been warm, but here in Connecticut, after a day of rain, it seemed bitterly cold.

They had driven until she thought they must have reached Canada, but it was still only Connecticut. Finally he had directed her off the turnpike onto back country roads. He must have been sleepy himself and afraid to trust them while he dozed.

They had wound through darkness until they reached a spot that was deserted enough to suit him. She had to sleep sitting up at her seat under the wheel. There was no room for them all to lie down. She leaned against the window and felt the cold on the side of her head.

It was not as bad for the children. They lay on the rear deck, which was carpeted, and they had an old beach blanket to cover them. She took a sympathetic pleasure in their relative comfort.

The big man had the back seat to himself. It was only she and the younger man who had to sit.

She drifted in and out of frantic dreaming. She dreamed of home, and Ted. Of her childhood in New Jersey, and her father, who had died. She barely remembered him, but he was alive in her dream. She had not known at the time of his death that he left them a profitable business, which her mother later sold.

She woke with the certainty that she should tell the men to ransom her. That her mother would pay anything. That she was more valuable alive than dead.

After she had been awake for a while, she knew it wouldn't work. They would not want to go back to New York to arrange a pickup, especially as they already had money from the bank. Distance was what they needed now. And there was no guarantee that they would return her alive, even if her mother paid a ransom.

She slept again, and woke because she was cold in her thin corduroy jacket. She thought the night had grown lighter. It was still too dark to see her watch.

Beside her, leaning against his own window, the man sighed and mumbled.

She didn't even know his name.

She tried to stretch her legs, to unkink her body. She was sleepless now and impatient to be doing something.

He mumbled again. The sky really had grown lighter. Then the seat moved as he woke and shifted his position.

He scrambled for his gun.

She said, "Don't worry, I'm still here."

In the dim light, his face looked pale and young. He was probably younger than she was.

She wanted to ask what would happen when they reached Vermont. She knew he wouldn't answer, and if he thought she was anxious, he would torment her with it.

"What time?"

She said, "I can't see, but I think it's getting near dawn."

He opened his window and looked out. "The rain stopped."

"Yes. I hope it's sunny and warm today. I'm freezing."

It was ridiculous to converse this way with someone who had kidnapped her and probably intended to kill her.

"Let's get going, huh?" He turned to the back seat. "Hey, Torrey."

So that was the big man's name.

Torrey grunted, and his mouth made a chewing motion.

"Before we start," said Kate, "could I . . . It sounds

silly, out here where there isn't any bathroom, but that's what I'd like to do."

"You want to pee?"

"Well, yes. You have a charming way of putting it, but that's basically what I meant."

Their voices woke the children. Darren cried, "Mommy?"

"Yes, baby, I'm here."

Candy whimpered, "I'm cold. I want to go home."

"Me, too." Darren's voice had a hoarse, unhealthy sound.

"You want to pee," said the man, "go ahead. But I'm right here with this stubby. I'm not taking it off you." He meant the gun.

"If you don't mind, I'd like some privacy."

"I'd like some privacy," he mimicked.

"Do you really think I'd try to escape when you have my children?"

"Okay, lady, get it over with. Go in the woods there, but you better come back in a couple of minutes." He checked his watch. "Three minutes, or that's it for the kids."

She hurried into the woods, glancing over her shoulder to be sure they were not driving off with the children.

It was only a small, thin wood. There would be no privacy after all.

Finally she found a thicket of brambles and hid behind it. She looked about for some way to leave a message. No one would see it there. No one but the men. Besides, they had given her no time.

She went back to the car, and each of the others took a turn. The big man stood next to a tree in full view of the children.

She felt dirty and disheveled, and her brain was numb. Would there ever be a chance? They should reach Ver-

54

mont in a matter of hours. After that, they wouldn't need her anymore.

Backing out of the wooded area, she followed a road that ran past picturesque farms and more woods. She thought of all the people on those farms, people leading normal lives. What would they think if they knew that a carful of hostages was passing by? Would they run to the window and look out?

"Where am I going?" she asked.

"Keep on till we get to a drive-in. Then you're going to look at that map and find some way to Vermont."

Again she felt a strange, misplaced gratitude, almost a camaraderie, which she could not understand. At least he was taking care of her and the children, letting them eat—whatever he planned to do in the end.

They passed a horse farm with paddocks that looked like green velvet surrounded by white rail fences. And another farm, large and prosperous, with extensive barns, silos, and rolling pastureland. Walled estates with long driveways and invisible mansions.

"I doubt if there are any drive-ins on this road," she said.

"Keep going. There'll be a town somewhere."

She drove on for mile after mile. They must have crossed the whole state of Connecticut, and then some.

Finally the houses became smaller and closer together. They were coming to a village. It turned out to be a picture-pretty village with no fast-food restaurants. Not even a gas station. The man said nothing, and soon the village was behind them.

Her eyes burned with fatigue. On and on . . .

After a while she became aware that he was staring at her. She glanced at him and then back at the road.

"So your old man's in Chicago," he said. "What happened, he got enough of you?"

"He's on a business trip." It didn't matter now if she talked.

"How long?"

"Just this weekend. He's coming back tonight."

The man digested that information. She wondered if it had been wise to let him know. He might decide to do away with them before the search could begin.

She was too tired to retract or qualify it. Let him think what he liked.

"Going to be a surprise for him, isn't it?" he said.

"It certainly is."

"You ever play around when you were married?"

She flinched, thinking of the children. Would they know what that meant?

Then it occurred to her that it might be a way of staving off any sense of urgency, if only she could figure out how to manage it. Her foggy mind could no longer fit two ideas together.

"He might think that," she said. The man appeared satisfied.

They were entering a larger community, a more commercial one. They passed a diner and a Lobster Inn.

"Slow down," he said. "There's McDonald's up there. See if it's got a drive-in."

It had. She took her place in the line. Immediately a small truck drove in behind her. She looked back to see a blond teenager and heard his radio playing. He gazed out of the window, beating time to the music on his steering wheel. He noticed nothing, couldn't feel her fear radiating out to him.

She scarcely felt it herself. It was no longer fear. It was only a dullness, a resignation.

That's bad, she thought, but couldn't rouse herself.

Beside her, the man leaned over to accept their order, pushing against her, his whiskers brushing her cheek. He spoke genially to the girl in the window, then made Kate drive to the far side of the parking lot. She would not be able to look out at the passersby or in any way attract their attention.

He had ordered a hearty breakfast for her, but she could barely swallow.

"You better eat," he said.

She set down her Egg McMuffin. "Would you feel like eating if you were me?"

His voice hardened. "You're alive, aren't you? What else do you want?"

He didn't understand. Didn't even see her as a human being.

"You keep calling me 'lady,' " she said. "Wouldn't it be easier if you knew my name? It's Kate."

"So what?"

"I thought—so you'd have something to call me."

He might be incapable of seeing anyone as a human being. Perhaps even himself.

"I just mentioned it, since we seem to be spending a lot of time together."

She did not dare ask about him. He would probably feel threatened by a personal question.

"My husband's name is Ted," she went on. "And my children are Candace and Darren. We call my daughter Candy for short."

"Those are some fancy names."

"Well, my name isn't fancy. I don't think Kate is fancy, do you? And Ted isn't, either."

"What's that short for?"

"Edward. His mother liked 'Ted' better than 'Eddie.' "

Ted was such a cuddly name. She closed her eyes, feeling an ache.

He didn't even know she was gone. Wouldn't know until tonight. Nine, ten o'clock, he had told her. His flight. Long after she reached Vermont. Long after—

"You seem to be an intelligent person," she said.

57

"I get by."

"Did you ever do anything like that before?"

"Like what?"

"The bank thing."

"Shut up, will you?"

"You're right, I talk too much. That's how I got into trouble in the first place, isn't it?"

"How would I know?"

He really didn't know. He seemed to have no idea how she had ended up here. Probably, in his eyes, it had nothing to do with him. He was probably a psychopath, unable to see anything beyond his own wants and needs. Unable to experience other people as real.

She drank her coffee, although it burned her tongue, and forced herself to finish the Egg McMuffin. The rest of the food she distributed to the children. They ate and were almost placid. They probably couldn't see, as she could, where it was all leading.

The man gobbled his own breakfast and unfolded a map. "Find how to get to Vermont," he told her.

"Where do you want to go in Vermont?"

His foot twitched. "Just get to Vermont! Find the way from here."

Darren muttered, "Don't talk to my mommy that way."

"It's okay, Darren," she said quickly. "He has a gun, so he can talk any way he wants."

Her sarcasm was lost on the men and probably on the children. She busied herself with the map. It took a minute or two to figure out just where they were. The man grew impatient and twitched again.

"This one, I think." She pointed to a long red line. "It goes off the map, but I know Vermont's up here someplace."

"Don't you have any other maps?" He rummaged an-

58

grily through the glove compartment, discarding Long Island, New York, and New Jersey.

"Not in there. The ones we don't use often, we keep at home."

"Yeah? That's real smart."

"But—I wasn't expecting this."

He grunted and folded the map. "So you know where you're going, right?"

"I think so."

"You better be sure."

"I am. Really."

She wasn't, but dared not say so. It would make him furious. So would getting lost. But getting lost might gain her a little more time.

"What's the big thing with Vermont?" she asked.

"None of your business."

"Okay, but I feel as if we're driving off the edge of the world. I don't know where we're going or why."

"You don't have to know."

"It's not a very populated state. Is that why? A lot of empty space?"

There was no answer.

"Wouldn't it be easier to hide in a crowd?" she asked.

"Nope. They watch the cities. Too many cops around."

It seemed to remind him of something. He turned on the radio. At the point where they had set it yesterday, there was nothing. He jiggled the tuning knob.

"I doubt if you can get that station up here," she said.

He flipped through the entire range. There were snatches of rock, country music, commercials.

"You probably can't get it," she repeated. "We're far away from New York now."

"Then what the hell good is it?" In a fury, he twisted the knob back and forth. The sound came out in gasps and chokes.

"Take it easy!" she cried. "It's not made to pick up stations from far away. You just can't do it."

"I want the New York news!"

"But it can't—"

He yanked at the knob. It came off in his hand. He kicked the floor. Seizing his gun by the barrel, he hammered at the radio, smashing its dial. Hammered . . . hammered . . . hammered . . .

In the mirror, she could see her children's faces. Now they were beginning to understand. She gripped the steering wheel and stared at the road.

Chapter Seven

Several times, she nearly drove off the road.

How can I sleep, she wondered, *on my last day?*

It was a sunny day. She tried to savor every moment, but all she felt was a dull lassitude.

They were driving over a mountain road in Vermont. The Green Mountains, he told her with a smile. He was probably glad to be getting there, but the smile made her uneasy.

"That's what 'Vermont' means," she ventured. "Green Mountain."

They had stopped for lunch several hours ago. Again she couldn't eat. He had become irked and pointed the gun at her.

"I don't like skinny women," he had said.

She hadn't thought about it then. She had been too upset at having to force down an unwanted hamburger. Now she wondered what he meant by it. Was he talking about her?

"Hey, stop!"

She braked, throwing them all forward. Her heart pounded. She hadn't even looked to see if anything was behind her.

The big man snarled, "You dumb or something?"

"He said to stop." Her voice came out in a thin thread.

"You dumb, Lowell?"

The younger man ignored him. "Back up a little. Go in that road there."

She hadn't seen it. On their right, a little way back, was a narrow dirt lane overgrown with weeds.

"I can't get the car in there. It's not even a road any more."

"I said go in."

She backed the car and cautiously turned onto the bumpy, rutted track.

"How do you know it goes anywhere?" she asked.

"Just drive, okay?"

If the car bogged down or broke an axle, he would probably blame her. She bumped and scraped her way forward, trying to see through the weeds, to avoid the deepest ruts, the largest stones. Branches along the side of the road screeched against the paint.

They drove over a low hill. There the road ended in the middle of a field. She stopped the car.

Lowell muttered angrily, cursing to himself. "Too open."

She did not know what he meant or what she was supposed to do.

"What are you waiting for?" he demanded.

"Instructions."

"What are you, stupid? I said it's too open. Let's go!"

She turned her car and eased back through the weeds and ruts to the highway.

Here and there along the road were houses, some large and some small, some obviously vacation cottages. The area was more built up than he probably expected. He tapped his foot as he watched out of the window, twisting his head from side to side.

After a while he stopped her again. There was another dirt road, this time to the left.

She thought it was as bad as the first one. Maybe worse. "If we wreck the car," she said, "we'll be stuck out here in the middle of nowhere."

"Shut up. I told you what to do."

Again the car bounced over rocks and into hollows and potholes. They rounded a bend and were out of sight of the highway. That was what he wanted.

"Hey, look!" He pointed ahead.

She saw nothing but trees.

The car sank into a hole. She stepped on the gas.

"I hope we don't break something," she said.

"Hey, Torrey, look at that! You see that?"

Now she could see it, too. It was a large, gray, ramshackle barn with a collapsing roof. It rose above low trees, until they rounded the last bend and found themselves in a clearing.

The barn was surrounded by meadow grass. Beyond it, the mountain sloped away, and she could see other rolling hills in the distance. Part of the slope was occupied by an orchard gone to weed, neat rows of old, worn-out trees, many of which appeared dead. In front of it was the stone foundation of a house.

Golden afternoon sunshine spilled over the scene. A warm breeze rippled the tall grasses.

"This is the place," said Lowell.

Torrey did not agree. "It's too open."

"Watch her." Lowell got out of the car and walked to the barn.

Its gaping entrance, large enough to admit a wagon or a tractor, seemed to swallow him. Did he mean this as a hideout?

Soon he reappeared, smiling broadly.

"You can drive right in there," he said.

She looked up at the sagging roof, the paneless windows. "There are probably nails and broken glass."

63

"I said drive in."

Slowly, she lurched over hummocks of grass. The children sat forward, watching intently.

The end of the line.

She bumped up onto a floor. After the clear, bright sunshine, the darkness of the barn's interior blinded her. She could see only Lowell, standing in front of her, motioning her forward.

She could run him down. Run right over him.

Lowell directed her into a front corner, so the car could not immediately be seen through the open door. After she had parked and turned off the engine, he took the keys from her.

She heard Torrey open his door and heave himself out. The children followed. Kate swung her legs from under the wheel and stood up.

Here it would happen. Here in this sunny, dead place, where outside the barn a butterfly dipped among the weeds.

The men conferred and explored, looking into the empty stalls. Candy huddled close to her mother. "It's cold in here."

Darren asked, "Are we going to stay here?"

"I don't know. We have to do what they tell us."

"Because they have a gun?"

"We can't stay here forever," said Candy.

"No, I don't see how we can."

"Are they going to kill us?"

"Of course not." She smoothed back Candy's hair. A six-year-old didn't really understand death. Its irreversibility.

Lowell came toward them. She had to make him realize the craziness, the futility, of what he was doing.

"This used to be a farm," she said brightly. "Too bad it doesn't produce any more."

"What are you talking about?"

64

"If you're planning to stay here, how are you going to live? You'll have to go out and buy food, and then they'll see the car."

"We got time."

Because Ted was not yet home. The car had not been reported missing, and neither had she. It was the car that would be spotted. Its color, make, and plate number.

"Well," she said, "I guess you know what you're doing."

"I guess I do."

She turned away from him and wandered across the dark barn floor. For twenty-four hours, she had had little chance to stretch her legs.

The floor was part wood and part earth, where the wood had rotted away. The barn smelled of damp earth and mustiness.

And it was cold, away from the sunlight. It would be much colder at night. They couldn't really mean to stay here without food, warm clothes, or bedding. Even water. If he knew what he was doing, it must have been a long-range plan.

Maybe they would steal another car, and then another. They could keep changing cars, and change their clothes. They might grow beards and dye their hair. It could be done.

And she and the children would be long dead.

The children hurried after her. Darren clutched at her hand. "Mommy, don't go away."

"I'm not going anywhere," she said. "I'm just looking around. Don't you know I wouldn't go off and leave you?"

"Promise?" asked Candy.

"Of course I promise."

Darren noticed a flight of steep wooden steps that led up to the barn's second story. "Where does that go?"

"I don't know barns very well," said Kate, "but I guess

it's a loft or something. Maybe a hayloft."

"Can we go up?"

"Not by yourselves. Not unless they say it's all right."

Darren looked back at Torrey, who seemed to be following them. "Can we go up there?"

Torrey, in turn, glanced at Lowell. Each of the men had already climbed partway up the stairs and taken a look.

"There's nothing up there," said Lowell, but he started toward the stairs. Kate took it as permission.

"Careful," she told the children. "Those steps are old. They might be weak."

Several boards felt loose, but the stairs held even under the weight of the men, who followed her closely. They found themselves in a large, bare room with a sagging roof and several smaller rooms at the back. In one place, the floor had fallen through, leaving a large, jagged hole.

The front end of the loft was wide open. The farmers had pitched their hay through that opening. She saw hinges and knew there had once been a closing of some kind.

Candy whimpered again, "I'm cold."

"I know," said Kate, "but try not to complain. We have to be careful not to make them angry."

Lowell went over to the open end and stood surveying the ground. If Torrey hadn't been there, she could have pushed him out.

She lowered her eyes. Torrey was watching her. If he had any brains, he could figure out what she was thinking.

He nodded his approval. "You've got real nice tits."

Her face flared. The children stared at her.

"Thank you," she answered coldly.

Of course he couldn't see anything under her jacket. It was the same as an obscene phone call. It gave him a thrill.

"You're not very friendly," he said.

"It depends on the circumstances. I don't consider kidnapping an occasion for friendliness."

"You don't have much choice, lady."

"That's it exactly. Coercion doesn't turn me on. And as I already told your friend, my name isn't 'lady.' "

"What's it matter?" He took a step toward her. She drew back.

Her rejection angered him. His eyes grew hot.

At that moment, Lowell turned around.

"Can't see anything from here." He sounded pleased. It meant nobody could see them.

"Better be friendly," Torrey muttered.

Lowell looked from one to the other and understood. He said nothing.

As they went back down the stairs, she felt Candy watching her. Candy knew something was going on.

Darren said, "I don't like it here. There's nothing to do.

"You can tell yourself stories," Kate replied.

"Mommy, can I have the blanket?" asked Candy.

"If they say it's all right."

"I want the blanket, too," said Darren. He added, "I'm hungry."

"You just had lunch," Candy reminded him.

"No, I didn't."

"Mommy, is tomorrow Monday? I'm going to miss school."

Tomorrow's Monday. Ted will be home tonight.

"I think we're going to miss a lot of things," said Kate.

Chapter Eight

The sun was low in the sky as they drove home from the airport. Ted felt as though he were racing against it. He drove at a normal speed, but it amused him to wonder if he could reach home before it went down.

"You're feeling a bit guilty, aren't you?" Elaine said as they entered Saltport. "That's why you wanted to catch the earlier flight."

So she had noticed. Maybe his speed wasn't so normal after all.

"Could be," he replied.

"I think I do, too. But, really, people do that kind of thing all the time. It's just new for us."

"Is it?"

She glared at him. "Of course it is! Do you think I make a habit of fooling around with married men? I got carried away. That's a tribute to you, Ted."

"I didn't know."

"Anyhow, it's over. I guess we were both a little bombed."

"A little."

"If it's all the same to you, it never happened, okay?"

"That will certainly make it easier at the office," he said.

He stopped the car in front of her building, but she did

not get out. After considering for a moment, she leaned over and kissed him.

He caught her. Held her.

It was only for now. The end of the weekend. She would understand that it was not a commitment.

"Whoa," she said, pulling away from him. "Somebody might see us."

"Does anybody here know us? Besides your mother?"

"They know me, and I don't want a lot of dumb questions. See you tomorrow."

He took her bag from the trunk and carried it into the lobby. She gave him another quick kiss on the cheek. When he went back to his car, the sun was still above the horizon.

He felt in a daze after that last embrace. He needed to rearrange his mental state. Prepare for Darren to climb up his leg. For Candy to ask if he had brought her anything.

He drove past the Brookside Mall and into Belle Harbor. Down Elton Avenue and Arnold Carver Road, and finally Oyster Drive.

Kate's car, he noticed, was already put away for the night. He could leave his outside, which suited him fine. He glanced at the house and wondered why the door had not flown open. They were probably watching TV.

Then he looked at the house again. It was a warm day, but all the doors and windows were closed.

It took people, especially kids, a while to get used to the spring. It took them even longer to learn to close up in the fall. Every year it happened. What could he do?

He locked his car and started up the walk. They must have heard him by now, but still the door didn't open. He began to wonder if they were even home. It was nearly dusk, and no lights were on.

He found the front door locked. That proved it. They weren't here, but where the hell would they be? He fished in his pocket, trying to find the key. He rarely had to use it.

Some homecoming this was turning out to be. He shouldn't have told her he would be late. Nine or ten o'clock. It was only to keep her from wanting to drive him to the airport.

He unlocked the door and pushed it open. "Anybody home?"

There was no answer. He did not hear the television or the children squabbling. Suddenly he missed that squabbling, interrupted by "Daddy! Daddy's here!" and the thundering of feet.

Airport. She wouldn't have gone to meet him! He had caught an earlier flight, but she didn't know which one he had planned to take. She couldn't be trying to meet every incoming flight from Chicago at all the different terminals. Nobody would do a thing like that.

He didn't think he had even told her which airport. It was usually Kennedy, because that was closest, but flights from Chicago were more apt to arrive at LaGuardia or Newark. Maybe she didn't know that, but how could she assume anything, when New York had three airports?

He went through the kitchen, noting that it was neat, clean, and in order, and opened the door to the garage. Her car was not there.

"Damn it, Kate, if you've gone to the airport, you're an idiot. I hate to say it, but that's what you are."

He took his bag upstairs and unpacked it, flinging the laundry into a pile on their bed. He took out all his annoyance on the laundry. If worst came to worst, he would wash the damn stuff himself. The machine would make a warmly busy sound in its little room next to the kitchen.

That was it, he decided. The house was too damn quiet. It didn't sound like home.

Kate sat in the open loft door and watched the sun go down. The children were snuggled next to her, one on either side. The men were downstairs, and she could hear sounds at the car, just below her. A clanking of metal. They were probably checking the well under the back deck to see what they could find.

She knew there wasn't much. Only a jack, a few tools, and a gallon jug of wiper fluid.

"Are they going to take the car and go away without us?" Candy asked.

"Probably not, but I wouldn't mind if they did."

"How would we get home?"

"We'd manage." She would not tell them how easy it would be. Because it wasn't going to happen.

"Daddy should be home soon," she said.

"I want to see him." Candy began to cry.

"You will. When he gets home and finds we're gone, he'll call the police. He'll give them the license number of the car, and then they'll look for it. And they'll find it, too, because we can't stay here without any food. We'll have to go out and get things."

Darren said, "I'm hungry."

Candy paused in her sobbing. "You're always hungry."

"I am not."

"Please don't fight with each other," said Kate. "Don't you think we have enough troubles already?"

Candy snuggled closer. "I'm sorry, Mommy."

"I'm sorry, too. For all of us."

In back of her, a floorboard crunched. Both men wore sneakers, but she had learned to distinguish Lowell's tread.

"Listen, baby," he told her. "As soon as it gets dark, you and me are going out to look for some food. The kids stay here."

"But I'm hungry," Darren protested.

71

Kate nudged him. "I'm sure he means for all of us. He hasn't been letting you starve, has he?"

"Are you going to bring it back here?" asked Darren.

She looked up at Lowell. His face was impassive, but that must have been what he meant.

"Are they staying alone?" she asked.

"My buddy'll be here."

"Oh. Great."

"What's that supposed to mean?"

"Nothing."

Damn it, what am I going to do?

When the sun had gone down, the air grew colder. After a long dusk, they watched the light fade and darkness fill the loft.

Finally he was ready to leave. She wished they could buy blankets and sleeping bags, but in any small village, all the stores would be closed by now.

Both children cried when she left. The barn was dark, and they had no light. And if they were not afraid of Torrey, they probably should have been.

"Just go and wrap yourselves in the blanket and try to sleep," she told them. "We'll be back before you know it."

She really had no idea where they were going. It might be ten or twenty miles to the nearest village. They had passed one that afternoon, a long way back. She had not noticed how far it was.

As they settled in the car, Lowell held the gun conspicuously on his lap. Not taking any chances. What could she do, with her children held hostage? She started the engine. Her headlights blazed on the wall.

"Turn those off!"

"I can't possibly get out of here without lights."

He slapped her hand. "Keep 'em off till you're out on the road."

"I'll try." She switched them off, backed away from the wall and bumped down from the floor of the barn. Enough daylight remained so that she could follow the driveway through the break it made in the trees. If she hit a bush, she would know she had veered off the road.

"Is he going to behave himself?" she asked.

"Who, Torrey?"

"I don't trust him. He got fresh with me. I don't trust him with my children."

Lowell shrugged. "He's okay. He's not what you think."

"I hope you're right." She wondered how well Lowell knew him.

They reached the end of the dirt lane. She asked, "Which way? Right or left?"

He was suddenly agitated. "I don't care! Just keep moving."

"There's nobody out here to see us." She turned left onto the dark, empty highway. They had originally come from the right. She knew the last village on that side was very far away.

"Now may I use the lights?"

"That's what I said."

This lonely road—so different from Oyster Drive. From home.

Had Ted come back yet? What was he thinking?

She tried to picture the scenario. He would find the house empty. He would assume she had gone to visit her mother. Probably he would leave his car in the driveway, so he might not notice that hers was out of the garage. Even if he did, he would think she had parked at the station.

Would it enter his mind that she would never stay at her mother's very late or overnight when the children had school the next day? Did Ted even notice what went on in their household?

How soon would he think to call her mother and ask if she was there? Would they both worry together?

She did not know how many miles they had driven before she saw a cluster of lights down the side of the mountain.

"How do we get there?" she asked. "I don't find any road."

He told her to keep going. "There's got to be a way."

"Maybe we passed it. Or maybe there isn't any way from up here. It looks very steep."

They drove on for several more minutes. The lights were hidden now. The road was completely dark. She was sure there were bears in the woods.

She said, "I think we should go back to the village we saw this afternoon. At least we know it's there."

"Why didn't you go that way to start with?"

"I didn't know. And neither did you."

Her headlights picked up a spot where the shoulder was wide enough to turn the car. Neither of them spoke during the long drive back along the mountain ridge. She was not sure when they passed the road into the farm. She would never be able to find it again. Her children would be alone all night with Torrey.

After miles of darkness, she saw lights twinkling through the trees. The red of a neon sign. It was a restaurant perched on a slope above the road.

"Turn in there," he said.

He couldn't mean they were going to eat in a restaurant. It was too good to believe, in spite of her rumpled, wilted looks. There would be people around. Maybe she could get a message to someone.

He directed her to a far corner of the parking lot, under a tree.

"Give me the keys," he said, "and wait in the car. And don't try anything funny. Remember where your kids are."

There must be something she could do. Her mind worked furiously. She would stop somebody and tell them. . . .

He did not go into the restaurant. He took something from his pocket and crouched behind another car.

He was switching the license plates. So they would never be spotted, never found. He thought of everything, and she was trapped. Exhausted. A tear splashed onto her hand. She hadn't known it was there. Another tear fell and she was too tired to stop it.

Maybe someone would come out of the restaurant and see what he was doing. *Please, please, someone.*

She heard him working at the back of the station wagon. She could feel his bumps and thumps through the metal body. Then he transferred the wagon's plates to the other car.

When it was finished, he climbed in beside her. "Let's get moving, huh?"

They were not going to eat. It was a trick. She started out to the highway.

She couldn't see. The tears in her eyes distorted the lights, making rays shoot out in all directions. She tried to wipe them away.

"Turn left," he said. "It's a little ways ahead. And you better watch where you're going. If we don't get back in a couple of hours, you won't have any kids to worry about."

Oh, my God. Oh God, why hadn't they told her?

How could they do it? Had they made no allowance for being lost in the dark? Why had he stopped to change the plates?

Turn left. Away from the children. She pressed on the gas and drove as fast as she could.

He laughed. "That got you moving, huh?"

"It's not fair," she said.

"So what's fair?"

It wouldn't mean anything to him. All that mattered was what he wanted. She couldn't think. She could only concentrate on the dark, unfamiliar highway.

The road seemed endless. From time to time they passed a house, an isolated spot of light. After a while there were more lights, closer together. Thank heaven. They drove down a hill and reached the village they had passed that afternoon.

They cruised the main street, almost the only street. They found one small grocery store. It was closed for the night.

At the end of the street she noticed a cluster of lights. Strips of neon. Several parked cars.

"There's a diner," she said. "I think it's open."

"Hmm."

An uninterested grunt. He was already tired of spending his ill-gotten gains to keep three hostages alive.

"Let's go." He nodded toward the diner.

As they got out of the car, she ran her fingers through her hair to comb it. Lowell's hair was tousled, and golden whiskers covered the lower part of his face.

We're a real pair, she thought as they entered the diner. *Please, somebody notice.*

A few looked up and then went back to their eating. It felt strange to be among people. She was there with them, and yet apart, as though enclosed in a bubble.

Lowell placed his order. "Eight burgers to go," he said, "and make it quick."

"Anything to drink?" asked the woman behind the counter.

"You got beer? Okay, soda, then, in cans. Gimme five root beers."

"How do you want your burgers?"

"Whatever. Just hurry it up."

Please. Please.

If only they had found a McDonald's. But these burgers had to be cooked to order.

Two hours. Was it only two hours? Why hadn't he told her?

Please, somebody. Help me.

She looked around the diner. It had shiny gray walls, and Formica tabletops the color of tomato soup. She tried to catch someone's eye.

Why couldn't they tell? How could she be standing here, so close to all these people, and have none of them realize her danger?

"Do you want your burgers well done?"

"No, this is okay."

"They're only rare now."

"That's good enough. You got any ketchup?"

"On all of them? Do you want onions?"

"Forget the onions," he said. "Just ketchup."

They watched as the waitress wrapped each hamburger. She was deft and quick.

How many hours? There was a clock on the wall, but she could not remember when the sun had gone down.

Lowell picked up one of the bags and tucked it under his arm. He nodded to Kate. She was to carry the rest, because he needed a free hand for his gun. When they got into the car, he seemed to take forever arranging the bags on the seat between them.

She stood it for as long as she could, then gently reminded him, "You have the key."

He chuckled and mimicked, "You have the key."

"You took it from me, remember?"

In a mincing voice, he echoed, "You took it from me, remember?"

Dear God, the man is an overgrown child. An idiot.

She couldn't say any more. He would notice that her teeth were chattering. She could only wait.

Chapter Nine

His laundry was done, and they still were not home. It was nearly ten o'clock.

"Kate, for Pete's sake!" he called into the empty house. "Are you going to wait there all night? Do I have to go back and look for you?"

How would he know where to look? How did *she* know where to look? She didn't.

He denied his anxiety by continuing to shout.

"You idiot, why would you go and meet me when I already had a car? That makes two cars, and twice as much gas. Are you crazy?"

Her car was a guzzler, too, that big station wagon. She could be rattlebrained at times, but would she really do anything so dippy as go all the way to meet him when he had his own transportation, and she didn't know what flight he was on?

"Call Jeanette," he said, still talking aloud because the house was too quiet. He matched up the last pair of socks, then reached for the bedside telephone to dial his mother-in-law.

No good. He couldn't remember her number. He went downstairs to the kitchen, where Kate had it taped to the wall for the children, in case of emergency.

After eight rings, Jeanette answered breathlessly.

"I just got in the door," she gasped. "I had a ballet. How are you, Ted? You're back from Chicago? Did you get all motivated?"

Everybody thought it was hilarious.

"I got back a while ago," he said. "They're not home. You don't know if she was planning to meet me at the airport, do you?"

"I have no idea. She was going to call me this morning about a museum trip. I never heard from her."

He felt a chill and brushed it aside. It was absurd to think that anything might have happened. How could it, in this quiet suburb, with neighbors all around?

"Did you try calling her?" he asked.

"Of course not. I went by myself."

"She wanted to go to the airport." Again the chill. Could she have gone and had an accident? "I thought she might have tried to meet me, but she didn't know what flight I was taking, and I caught an earlier one anyway."

"I don't know what to say, dear."

"I know you don't. She must be out somewhere, but it's getting kind of late for the kids. I was sort of wondering—"

Another man? The thought made something flip over inside him. She was seeing a man and had left the kids with somebody, and he had no idea who.

"I'll get back to you, Jeanette. If you hear anything, give me a call, okay?" He hung up quickly.

The idea was preposterous. *Kate?* Not Kate.

But his thoughts raced ahead. If it were a casual thing, just a simple tryst, she would have aimed to be home before he was.

Unless she was trying to tell him something.

Or something happened. Car trouble, maybe. Even then, she could have gotten home, and picked up the car later. Unless the guy had a wife . . . Oh, hell.

But if she left the kids somewhere, wouldn't Candy

79

start to worry after a while and call home? Or did Candy know how to reach Kate? Were the children in on this, too?

He thought of the couple next door, the Ackermans. Friendly, older people. He looked up their number in the phone book.

What was her name? Doris?

"Hello, Doris, this is Ted Armstrong, your neighbor. Listen, I was away on a business trip this weekend, and I can't find my wife and kids. Would you happen to have any idea—?"

"No, I haven't," Doris replied. "I haven't talked to her at all. I did see them drive out yesterday. It was a little past noon, in all that rain. I couldn't imagine—"

"Did you see them go anywhere today?"

"No, I didn't happen to notice."

He had not meant to imply that she spent her day glued to the window.

"Would you know if they came back yesterday?" he asked. "I mean, were there any lights on, or anything?"

A tryst. Would she have kept the kids away all night?

Sure, she might have farmed them out to their friends. But who were their friends?

"No, I didn't." He heard Doris's voice raised, away from the phone. "Sam!" And then a shouted conversation. "Did you see any lights on in the Armstrong house last night? Did you really not, or you just didn't notice?"

"He says he didn't," she reported, "but that doesn't mean anything. You can't go by Sam."

"Thanks," said Ted.

He tried to sort it all out. Her mother hadn't heard from her. The Ackermans hadn't seen her since she drove out sometime yesterday.

Was it she who was driving, or had they only seen the car? But he hadn't found any dead bodies, so if it was

80

somebody stealing the car, they must have stolen her, too.

He shook his head to clear away the craziness, the melodramatic flights of fancy.

There were two possibilities. Either she had gone somewhere yesterday—maybe a boyfriend, maybe not—and hadn't come back, or she had come back and the Ackermans hadn't noticed, and she had gone to meet him at the airport and hadn't come back.

"Why the hell don't you come back?" he bellowed.

Maybe she had left him for good. He raced upstairs and checked through her clothes. He couldn't tell what was missing, but if anything, it wasn't much. He tried to remember the various outfits she wore. One by one he accounted for them. Maybe it was a rich guy who was going to buy her a whole new wardrobe.

But what had she done with the kids? Did the rich guy get them, too?

He thought of calling the police. It seemed a little premature. She would come home and find the house swarming with cops, and she would laugh at him.

What if they tracked her to another guy's place? Would he want to know about that? Hell, he couldn't call any of his friends, *their* friends, for the same reason. He didn't want to know.

Were they even now whispering about poor Ted?

He needed to talk to someone. Someone who was his friend, not Kate's, and who would care. At the moment, the only person he could think of was Elaine.

Feeling foolish, he looked up her number. He had rarely had occasion to use it.

"Ted!" she exclaimed, and he thought she sounded pleased. "What's up? Are you calling from home?"

"Yes, I am, and she's not here."

"Where is she?"

"I don't know. I thought she'd be here." He described

his homecoming, and some, but not all, of the things that had passed through his mind.

"I'd just relax, if I were you," she advised. "After a while the incoming flights will taper off and she'll come home, and you'll both be a little annoyed at each other, and then you'll forget about it."

"When do the incoming flights taper off?"

"I don't know. Try calling the airline. And stop worrying. Does anything ever turn out as bad as you think?" Her voice drifted into a yawn. "I'm not usually so tired this early."

"It was all those Bloody Marys on the plane," he said. "I'm feeling a little—"

He did not know what he was feeling. He paced the house and turned on the television. He kept looking at the clock and wondered when she would realize what a ridiculous thing she had done and come on home.

Or whether she had had an accident on the parkway.

They would let him know. They might have tried earlier, before he was home, but they'd try again.

He listened to the radio. There was no report of an accident. He supposed he could call the police, just to be sure. They would think: Poor guy, his wife's run out on him, and he won't admit it.

After a while, the radio beeped the hour. The television, which he had left on, began its eleven o'clock newscast.

Eleven o'clock.

He didn't know why he was so worried. It couldn't be anything serious, or they would have notified him by now.

He looked up his airline in the telephone book. The only number they gave for Kennedy Airport was a baggage service. He tried it and got no answer.

If she were waiting for him, and he didn't come, surely it would occur to her to try calling home. Anybody'd figure out to do that. Even Candy could figure it out.

He was fidgety. On edge. He couldn't settle down, and so he phoned Elaine again.

"Still not back?" she asked in a froglike croak.

"Did I wake you?"

"It's okay, Ted."

"I'm sorry, I wasn't thinking. I'm really sorry. I hope I'm not bothering your mother."

"No, she wears earplugs. Listen, Ted, do you want me to come over?"

"No, you go back to sleep. I'm sorry I bothered you." He was making a pest of himself, when he should have been able to handle this.

"It's okay, really. I wish I could help. But I'm sure it's all right."

"She hasn't even called."

"Maybe your phone's out of order. Maybe it doesn't get incoming calls. Want me to try?"

They tried it. The phone rang, and he heard her perfectly.

"I'm sure there's a reasonable explanation," said Elaine. "She's probably staying with a friend. Why don't you get some sleep?"

"How?" *What friend?*

"Bomb yourself out with a Bloody Mary. Pretend you're still on the plane and none of this is happening."

It was sound advice. In the liquor cabinet he found half a bottle of vodka, but there wasn't any tomato juice. He had to settle for a screwdriver.

With his second drink, he watched another round of news. Then he went to bed.

But he couldn't sleep. He lay awake, listening for the sound of her car.

Chapter Ten

She would never find the farm again. The children would die. She had been this way only once before and hadn't really noticed the landmarks. Now, in the dark, there were no landmarks.

"Speed up," said Lowell. "You're going to get attention."

"There's nobody to get attention *from*. If you'd help me look—"

"It's up ahead someplace."

He didn't care. Not about her children. Maybe they were already dead. Maybe Torrey had instructions.

There. She was sure that gap in the weeds was the first road they had tried that afternoon. The other was a little way beyond it, on the left. She slowed again.

"It's up there," he repeated impatiently.

"I know."

"Right there."

Thank God.

"Put out your lights."

Yes. So as not to call attention to the farm road.

"Keep moving!" he roared.

"I can't see!"

"Damn it, I told you keep moving."

She plunged blindly ahead. If the car bogged down, she would get out and run to the barn.

Finally they entered the clearing. The barn loomed black and silent.

Lowell found a flashlight in the glove compartment. They needed it as soon as they were inside. The darkness was thick. Opaque.

"Mommy!"

And Torrey's voice: "Shut up, you." She heard a slap. The flashlight skimmed their faces. Both children stood shivering on the steps.

"It's all right," she told them. "Everything's all right." Candy hugged her. "Mommy, I'm cold."

They were all cold. The men debated between themselves and concluded that a small fire on the earthen part of the floor would not be seen from the road. They went out to gather fallen branches and dry leaves from the orchard and started them burning with Torrey's cigarette lighter.

The floor was chilly, and the fire too small to give much more than illumination. Even with the blanket wrapped around them, the children shivered.

Kate passed them their hamburgers. "I'm afraid these are cold by now, but at least it's food."

Darren bit into his and made a face. "It 's icky. It's all pink meat."

"I know," said Kate. "We didn't have time—"

Lowell made a lunge toward the boy. "What do you want? You get free food, and you don't like it? Gimme that."

He grabbed for the hamburger. Darren rolled away from him, keeping it out of his reach.

"Stop it!" Kate screamed. "Leave him alone, you creep! You're the one who dragged us here, it's not his fault. If it weren't for you, he could be home in bed, eating a decent meal!"

Lowell had risen to his feet. He stood looking down at her and breathing hard. The children cowered, waiting to see what he would do. Torrey watched in fascination.

The fight drained out of her.

"I'm sorry. Darren, please don't complain. I know it isn't cooked the way you like it, but we had no time to wait. We did the best we could, so *please*."

She felt an unreasoning anger toward the children. Why couldn't they try to understand?

Darren's face was frozen, the bite still in his mouth, unchewed and unswallowed. Her fury vanished. In its place was a huge welling up of love. She wanted to hold him forever but was afraid to move.

"He's only a baby," she told Lowell in a choked whisper. "He's only four years old."

Lowell continued to stand. Finally he folded his legs and sat down.

"You'd better watch it," he said. "You all just better watch it."

Torrey popped open a soda can. The moment had passed, and he seemed disappointed.

Lowell finished his two hamburgers and sat staring into the fire. He fed it a twig to keep it going. Torrey, gulping down his drink, crushed the can with his fist, then got up and strolled outside.

The children were growing sleepy. She thought of putting them into the car, but it was warmer there by the fire, an oasis in the damp night air.

She watched the firelight on Lowell's face and was afraid of what he might be thinking. She wished Darren hadn't annoyed him. It wouldn't matter to Lowell that he was only a baby.

After a while he looked over at her. "I guess I sort of snapped."

She waited, still dreading. It seemed incredible that he would apologize.

"It's all right," she said finally.

"The kid made me think of something. Somebody."

"What do you mean?"

"My brother. He made me think of my brother Joey." Lowell took a stick from the fire and used it to rearrange the branches so they would burn better.

"How old is your brother?"

"He's dead."

"Oh. I'm sorry."

"They made like it was my fault."

"Who did?"

"My mom and dad. I was supposed to look after him. He was younger than me."

She had not really thought of Lowell as a human, feeling person. He had given her no reason to. Now he was talking about a family, a lifetime. A private grief, or grievance.

"How old were you?" she asked.

"I don't know. Eleven, maybe. Joey was seven. Alice was six."

"Your sister?"

"I had to walk them home from school, the both of them. Every day I had to. Joey was bad news. You couldn't do anything with that kid. He never listened. We got across the street, and he said he dropped something. I yelled at him not to go back, because the light changed and all the cars and trucks were coming, but Joey ran back in the street and got hit by a car. I remember him flying up in the air."

She could almost see it happen. The little boy who wouldn't listen, running out into the street.

"But that wasn't your fault," she said. "Couldn't they understand?"

"I just told you."

"What did they expect you to do?"

"It was mostly my dad. He hated me after that. Maybe he wished I was dead, too."

She felt an ache for the child who wasn't loved. The family scapegoat.

But that child was Lowell—the man destroying *her* family.

"What about your mother?" she asked.

He shrugged. "Maybe she didn't want to see me dead, but she wouldn't stand up for me, so I guess she blamed me, too."

"But your sister was there. Couldn't she tell them what happened?"

"She was just a kid. Anyhow, they know what happened. It's like they had to take it out on somebody."

"Well, maybe that's true. But maybe they didn't realize what they were doing. They were probably immature people, all wrapped up in their own feelings, just the way you were in yours—"

"Don't give me that psychology shit."

He obviously wanted an ally. Someone who would accept the excuses he made for himself.

"They always gave me a hard time," he said. "My dad drinks a lot, and he gets mean. Even sober, he's not too nice."

More excuses, even though it was probably true. He pushed the fire together, making the flames grow taller. The fire seemed to fascinate him.

"We had an apartment," he went on, "back home. We were on the fourth floor. One time my dad got so drunk he fell all the way down to the third floor, down the stairs. I looked at him down there and I thought he was dead. A lot of times I wished he was dead."

"Do you still live with your parents?"

"Shit, I got out of there years ago."

"What did you do?"

"Different things."

"How old are you?"

"Twenty-five. Why?"

Four years younger than she was. At twenty-five she had been a mother and an adult. She had worked, put her husband through school, was raising a child and giving birth to another. And Lowell—what was his purpose? Did he really have one?

"The trouble is," she said, "that no matter what's happened to you, no matter what people have done, or you think they did, you still have to take responsibility for yourself. And that's where you failed."

He gave her a long, steady look. It was a look that mocked her, and she knew she hadn't reached him. She had not really thought she could.

Chapter Eleven

She woke, hugging Candy for warmth. Her left side ached. She had slept in the same position all night, on the hard deck of the station wagon.

She tried to ease the ache, but there was no room to move. She was afraid of waking the children.

It was daylight. Just beginning to be daylight. Maybe five or six o'clock.

What was Ted thinking? Was he awake? Had he been awake all night? Or had he slept, thinking she was visiting a friend? Had he tried calling her friends?

She thought of her bed, and getting up in the morning, and smelling coffee as it gurgled in the machine, and sending the children off to school: Candy with her friends, and Darren with his car pool. On Wednesday it was her turn to drive the car pool. In two more days, it would be Wednesday.

I'm here, she thought. *I'm really here. This is real.*

What would happen? She pictured the days passing, and then weeks. Spring turning into summer. Would they be dead by then, buried in that orchard, where no one would ever find them?

Ted would always wonder. He would spend his whole life wondering what had happened to them.

Would he, after a while, have her declared dead? Would he marry someone like Elaine?

Would he have other children? Would he forget?

She tried to send him a message: *Ted! Ted, listen to me. I'm here in Vermont. I'm in a broken-down farm in the Green Mountains. Here. Are you listening?*

She waited, and knew it hadn't worked. Telepathy never worked except for other people, in books.

If she could move just a little, and take the weight off her hip. . . . The whole bone ached, radiating pain through her body.

At least the men had let her sleep in back with the children and the blanket. They had the softer seats, but no blankets.

She squirmed, trying to shift her weight. Candy murmured and opened her eyes. Then Darren woke.

In the front seat, Lowell sat up. "What the hell's going on?"

Gratefully, she sat up, too. She surrendered herself to shivering. The cold was everywhere, all through her. There was no warmth at all. She could not remember what it felt like to be warm.

Candy leaned her face against Kate's arm. "It's like a nightmare," she whispered.

Kate hugged her and said nothing.

They were all awake. Torrey and Lowell got out of the car.

Darren asked, "What are we going to do today?"

"I don't know, sweetheart. That's up to them."

"I don't want to stay here."

"I want to go home," said Candy.

"So do I," said Kate. "Very much. But we can't. They won't let us." How could she make the children fully understand their circumstances? They were probably waiting for her to do something about it.

91

Darren had to go to the bathroom. The men were not in sight. She couldn't ask permission. She and the children left the car and went outside.

Candy looked up at the rosy sky. "It's not even morning yet."

"The sun's on its way," said Kate. "Then it will get warm."

And burn off the dew, which made everything chillier. A little more chill, she thought, and the dew would be frost.

They rounded the side of the barn and encountered Lowell. "Where the hell do you think you're going?" he demanded.

She explained where they were going and hoped he wouldn't follow.

He stood watching them as they went on to the back of the barn. He didn't follow, but he was waiting in the same place when they returned.

She wondered if he had expected her to try to escape unseen through the trees and scrubby bushes at the back. How far could she have gotten before he came after them with his gun?

Trying to appear friendly, to show that he could trust her, she asked, "Do you think there's any water around here? I feel so dirty."

He sneered. "I really apologize I didn't get you the Waldorf Astoria."

Her friendliness grew ragged. "We have water at home. You could have left us there."

"Tough shit, lady."

"Do you mind if we look around a little? Maybe we can find something."

"Yeah, sure. Find a nice little potty, and hot and cold running."

She felt stung by his perpetual scorn. Couldn't he see that she was an intelligent person?

92

"I wasn't being unrealistic. I thought there might be a brook or something, or even a pond. Most farms have a pond of some kind. That's in case of fire. I always thought it was for the animals."

Chattering again. She did sound stupid.

He shrugged. She set off through the orchard, through damp grass and weeds, looking back to see if he would stop her. Instead he followed closely, his hand conspicuously arched over his pocket.

"Hey!" shouted a voice. Lowell spun about, drawing his gun.

It was Torrey. Lowell muttered a curse, then said, "Keep it quiet, you shit."

Torrey caught up with them. "What the hell's all this?"

"We're trying to find some water," said Darren.

Torrey stared over his head at Lowell. Kate caught the look that passed between them. It said more than she wanted to know. The two had been making plans. Torrey seemed to question why the hostages were still alive.

Lowell understood it, too. In a low voice, he said, "You can't drive without your glasses."

"Better than this," Torrey answered.

Meaning, she supposed, herself and the children. She wondered if Lowell could drive at all. She felt a shakiness begin in her arms and legs and move inward.

Lowell walked on. She followed, if only to get away from Torrey. The children, subdued, clung to her hands.

God, she thought, *do they know?*

At the far side of the orchard was a stone wall and then a woods. They found no water.

"Can we go look in the woods?" asked Candy.

"Sure, go ahead." Lowell sounded almost pleasant. As Kate started after them, he took her arm and held her back.

"They'll get lost," she said, her teeth beginning to chatter.

"Shut up." He pulled her close to him. He massaged her waist, and then his hand crept under her shirt. He bent down and pressed his mouth against hers. She held herself stiffly.

The kiss became more demanding. He owned her and was asserting that fact.

Mustn't fight him. Must buy more time.

The only way to buy time was to keep him wanting more.

He wouldn't let her go. She could feel the hardness under his jeans. *Ted*, she cried, drowning. *Please, Ted.*

She managed to twist away from him as she heard the children's voices, coming back.

He thought he heard a noise and sat up. The room was already light.

Next to him, the bed was empty.

"Kate?"

It wasn't the clock radio that had waked him. He checked, and found he hadn't set it.

"Kate!"

Downstairs, he thought. She would be in the kitchen.

But it was not quite six o'clock. And her side of the bed had not been slept in.

He got up and looked in the children's rooms. Both were empty. Untouched. It was odd that she hadn't called. If she were spending the night somewhere, she would have called him.

Unless she didn't want him to know.

But how could he help knowing that she wasn't home?

Six o'clock. What was he supposed to do now? He couldn't start waking people at this hour to ask if they had seen her.

He decided to have breakfast first. A breakfast of cold

cereal, just like the kids. She wouldn't let him eat choles-terol. He started the coffee maker and went upstairs to shave.

Back in the kitchen, he turned on the radio. The Salt-port station. They played inane music and gave weather and traffic reports. Nothing about Katherine Armstrong. Or Candace or Darren.

So they must be somewhere around, since there were no grotesque accidents or reports of three people with amnesia.

He washed his breakfast dishes and put on his clothes. He kept looking out of the window, expecting to see her car come into the driveway.

What time was school? He didn't even know. He thought it might be eight-thirty for Candy and nine for Darren. By nine o'clock, he was supposed to be at work.

He telephoned Elaine.

"Still not back?" she asked in surprise. "I wonder what could have happened."

"So do I, and I don't know what to do. I'd feel kind of silly, calling the police."

"Why? What do you think the police are for?"

"But what would I tell them? I don't have any reason to think it's—anything."

"Foul play, you mean?"

He hadn't wanted to say it.

"Nothing's been disturbed. They'll ask that, you know. Her car's gone, but it's her car and she's a licensed driver."

"Maybe she went somewhere in the car," Elaine sug-gested, "and then something happened."

"I've had the radio on. There's nothing about any acci-dents. And they'd certainly tell me."

He had a momentary picture of a car burned beyond recognition. But they could still trace the car. There were numbers engraved on it.

"Are you coming into work?" she asked.

He didn't want to. He wanted to stay and wait, but he could wait all day, and it would drive him crazy.

"I guess so. I might be a little late, though. Maybe I'll wait until after nine."

After she had dropped Darren at school. Then she'd be sure to come home.

Unless she went back to her boyfriend.

He couldn't believe she had a boyfriend. Wouldn't he know? Wouldn't there be a few hints or clues?

But if it was anything else, she would have called.

Chapter Twelve

At eight forty-five, a car blew its horn outside his house. *Kate*, he thought, as he dashed to the front door.

A green station wagon stood at the end of the driveway. That was all it was, just a dark green station wagon. It seemed to be waiting for something, and so he went out to it.

He didn't know the woman inside. She was blond and pretty. She leaned across two seat-belted children and asked, "Is Darren ready?"

"Darren?" His voice went suddenly husky.

"Aren't you Ted Armstrong? I'm Judy Patman. I take the car pool on Monday."

"Car pool. To Darren's school." He was beginning to get the picture. She had expected Darren to be home. That meant Kate hadn't called her.

"Darren's not here," he said. "They, uh . . . the kids spent the night somewhere else. I'm sorry she forgot to tell you."

"That's okay. We all have our moments. It's nice to meet you, Ted." The green station wagon drove off.

He felt uneasy as he returned to the house. Maybe Elaine was right. Maybe it was time to call the police.

Still, he was aware of something lurking in the back of his mind, just around a corner. It was something she had said, and it might have had to do with Sunday night. Something that would explain the whole thing.

By nine-thirty, she still hadn't come.

He felt edgy and restless, the old adrenaline pumping. It was probably the strain of waiting, rather than fear. He wasn't afraid, even if there was a boyfriend. He decided he would rather have it be a boyfriend than an accident. That way, only his self-esteem would suffer. But he wasn't guiltless, either. Maybe he deserved this.

He would make a few phone calls and then leave. He called Jeanette.

This time Jeanette was alarmed. "Do you mean you don't know where she is? At *all*?"

"I thought you might know," he said, thinking that it sounded as though Jeanette blamed him. "I mean, I thought you might have heard from her since last night."

"Oh, Ted, I don't know what to say."

She had said exactly that when he last talked to her.

"Did you try calling the police?" she asked.

"No, I was just about to."

He called a few other people first, which was exactly what the police would have done, anyway. He called Betsy Fielder, one of her best friends. Betsy hadn't talked to her since Thursday. He tried the Hedwins, before he remembered that Lenore had a job now, and he didn't know where she worked.

Men friends? He couldn't think of any special men friends. They were all couples.

If she had a man friend, would she tell him about it?

The telephone rang.

Elaine's voice asked, "Any luck?"

"Any luck about what?"

"The police."

"I didn't call them yet. I've been calling friends. I know she said there was something she was going to do, if

98

I could just remember. I thought I might get a clue from talking to people."

"You know, Ted, if a person's really missing, the trail starts getting cold after twenty-four hours."

Another chill. He didn't want to be chilled. He wondered if he might be trying to deny the whole thing.

"I think she said she was going somewhere, and I don't remember which day. I didn't pay much attention."

He should have paid attention, damn it. He had been too full of his own trip, his own activities.

She often complained about that, too, saying that it meant he didn't care. That he thought everything she did was trivial and unimportant, which meant he didn't care about *her.* Could she have gone off with another man because of that? Someone who showed more interest?

Elaine asked, "Do you mean she was going somewhere to spend the night? And you don't remember?"

"I don't think it was to spend the night, but she might have decided to stay over. So I'll wait a little longer, okay?"

"She'd stay over, when you were coming back from a trip?"

"I don't *know*, you see. She might have been trying to shake me up a little. But that's why I want to give it more time."

"In other words, you refuse to be shaken up. I think you're nuts, Ted. I'd call the police."

"That's exactly what I'll do, if something doesn't happen soon. I'm going to work, and I'll try calling home now and then."

"Why is it," she demanded, "that men are so afraid to ask for help?"

He tried to think of an answer, but found he was talking to a dead phone.

❀   ❀   ❀

Lowell followed her up to the loft. She had to get away from him, but there was no place to go.

Darren skittered ahead of her and went to lean out the loft door. He liked the view from there, and the sunshine.

"Get back here!" she called.

He turned to stare at her, not understanding the anger in her voice. His puzzled face made her choke again with love.

Lowell seized her arm. "You're missing your chance, baby. We could make it, just you and me."

That was why she hadn't wanted Darren near the edge.

"I don't think you understand." She could not believe it was really happening, right now. It was all coming to a head. "I'm not going anywhere without my children. Whatever happens to them, happens to me, too."

She had said it. Her own death warrant. But it was sealed when she gave birth to the children, if this was their destiny.

He stared at her, and she saw that he really didn't understand. He had believed she would do anything to save herself. Now he merely thought she was stupid.

"It's your only chance," he said again. "My buddy wants to go on, get out of here."

She would die with the children. Have it over with. No. Not the children. No.

People like her—what did they do?

The children watched her. She saw that Candy understood too much. Her face was ashen. Even her lips had lost their color.

How? Kate looked around, assessing the barn.

The children clung to her. They depended on her, and she was helpless. Her eyes swept the loft door. Torrey was out there somewhere. The car . . .

If only she were stronger. She could knock him senseless and take the keys. But how? He knew she couldn't do it. He felt safe.

She ran through it anyway. She saw him crumple forward, saw herself reach into his pocket for the keys. Downstairs. The children. Into the car. She would have to back first. Torrey would come as soon as he heard the engine. Torrey had a gun.

She would have Lowell's gun. But how to fire it? Was there a safety catch? How?

So . . . helpless . . .

He still gripped her wrist. It had all happened in an instant. One brief moment of dreaming.

She heard Torrey on the stairs. Heavy, like a tank. His springy hair and then his shoulders rose above the floor. He was coming toward them. Almost there. She saw the gun in his hand and turned away quickly.

She made herself look into Lowell's eyes. Look, and not flinch.

"I'll go with you," she said, her throat tense, her voice unnaturally high, "if you'll take the children, too. That's the only way. We could—we could pretend we're a family."

"Shit," he said and flung away her hand.

"They'll never find you. They'll be looking for two men."

"Shut up."

"Huh?" Torrey moved closer to them. He smelled horribly of sweat.

She began to cry. She couldn't do it.

She took a deep breath and forced down the tears.

"Nothing," she told him. "I shouldn't have said anything."

"What the hell's going on?"

"Nothing. It's nothing."

It was all or nothing. This was her only chance, and she hadn't done it right.

She pulled Lowell aside and plunged on desperately.

"You could have me and all the money, too."

101

She said it so Torrey could hear her. Again she tried to meet Lowell's eyes. She saw his hand come up and saw the blow as it whipped toward her face.

"Mommy!" screamed Candy.

"Get away!" Distracted, thank God, so he wouldn't see her shock, her tears. She herded the children back toward the storage rooms, then remembered the hole in the floor.

"Just—stay there," she told them. Then, "Go down to the car. Wait in the car for Lowell and me."

It was all or nothing.

"The hell you do," breathed Torrey.

What if he shot the children?

"Go!" she screamed.

Lowell reached for his gun.

"I'm sorry, Lowell, I—"

She drew a sick breath. The gun was moving toward her, not Torrey.

Something slammed against her forehead. She reeled. The floor rippled and rose. The barn turned black.

In the distance, she heard their voices and a roaring in her head. Her numb hand reached out and touched the floor.

My babies, she thought. *My babies*.

Chapter Thirteen

A few people glanced up as Ted walked through the outer room toward his own office. It was about the same number, and the same people, who usually turned to look at anyone going by. That must have meant Elaine had kept his troubles confidential. He blessed her for it.

He had barely sat down at his desk when she came into the room.

"What's the latest?"

"I'm going to give it a couple more hours—"

"*Why*, Ted?"

"Because I know she told me something, if I could just remember what, and it's silly to get the police all alerted for nothing."

"Maybe it isn't nothing."

"It has to be. What could have happened? The house was neat and clean. No signs of mayhem." There, it was out. He hated even thinking it. But there hadn't been any.

"It's up to you," she said and left the room.

Darn right it was up to him. He sat staring at the pictures of the children on his desk. School pictures. Suddenly he had an idea.

The name of Candy's school. It wasn't Belle Harbor

Elementary, or anything simple like that. It was a person. A poet. Amy Lowell? Emily Dickinson? That might be it. He called directory assistance.

He had a little trouble, but since the public schools were all listed under one heading, it didn't take long to find Edna St. Vincent Millay.

Nobody called it that, of course. When he dialed the number he had been given, they answered, "Millay School, may I help you?"

"Is there any way to find out," he asked, "whether a particular child is in attendance today?"

They were suspicious. Because of child-snatching, he supposed. They had to be careful.

"I only want to know if she's there," he said and explained his reason. He felt ridiculous, not knowing where his own family was.

They transferred him to someone else. The principal. A Mrs. Wong. He had met her once last fall at the PTA, when Kate insisted that he take an interest in his children's education.

Mrs. Wong was more helpful than the secretary had been. He heard conversation, and she asked him to "hold on, please." After a minute or so, she returned to tell him that Candace had been listed as absent.

"Oh, no!" he said.

"Have you called the police?"

"I'm about to do that. I just thought if she was there at school, everything would be okay."

It still didn't have to mean anything. It could mean they had gone visiting and hadn't come back.

"I don't know what to do," he said, half to himself.

"I'd call the police," replied Mrs. Wong. "But you know your family better than I do."

He had discovered that he didn't really know his family at all. He didn't know their friends, or what they did with themselves when he was not around. He had not, until this morning, thought it was important to know those things.

But they were his family, and that made it important. And now it was too late.

Chapter Fourteen

Torrey was dead. But Lowell was very much alive.

He did not seem unduly disturbed by the fact that he had shot his companion to death. He did not blame himself and he did not blame Kate. It had been a stupid idea, trying to get them to kill each other. She had known it wouldn't work, but she had to try. It had almost cost her own life.

She sat in the loft, nursing her battered face. Lowell was somewhere outside, trying to dig a grave with the tools he had found in the car. The lug wrench, probably. You could break the earth with it. You could remove one of the hubcaps and use it as a scoop. She thought about that, and not of Torrey lying crumpled on the floor, his blood staining the rough wood. Of Lowell forcing her to help him drag the body to the loft door and throw it outside. The terrible *thunk* when it hit the ground.

It hadn't really struck her yet, the reality of it. The dead man, and that she was responsible for his death. It had been him or the children. Maybe herself. That was all that mattered.

"What's going to happen?" Candy whimpered, resting her head on Kate's lap.

"I don't know."

She could not believe any of it *had* happened. She, who had never seen a dead human before.

"Is he going to kill us, too?"

Kate did not answer. Candy began to sob.

"What will Daddy do without us?" And then, "Why doesn't he come and look for us?"

"He's probably looking for us right now," said Kate, "but he doesn't know where to look."

"Why can't we run away now, when Lowell's out there and he can't see us?"

"Because he has the keys to the car, and we couldn't get far enough on foot. He'd come after us with his gun."

"But what's going to happen? Are we going to stay here forever?"

Kate wondered if she knew what "forever" was.

"We'll just do what he says and try to keep calm. If we don't make him angry, we might have a chance."

"But I don't like it here."

"I'm sure he'll want to go on somewhere. To Canada, maybe."

And maybe, without Torrey, he would be more dependent on her, at least to drive the car.

Or maybe he would kidnap someone else.

"Hey, you!" Lowell called from below. "Get on out here."

He was standing by Torrey's body.

"Me?"

Not the children. Not yet.

He jerked his head impatiently. "Get out here and give me a hand."

She tried to walk. Her head spun and her legs buckled.

"Mommy, I don't want you to go!"

"It's all right," she said. "You just wait here. Don't get him upset."

"Will you come right back?"

"As soon as I can."

Gripping the wall, she made her way downstairs. He was annoyed that she had taken so long.

"I have a little trouble walking," she explained. "You hit me pretty hard, do you know that?"

He made her carry Torrey's legs. She picked them up and tried not to look or think about it.

The grave was around at the side of the barn, where the hill began to slope toward the valley. That wasn't good, she thought. The topsoil would wash off. He should have put it on level ground.

It was not deep. He hadn't used a hubcap to dig with, she noticed. He had mostly scraped the earth away.

They dropped Torrey into the grave and found he was too long for it. They had to double his legs at the knees. She swayed, feeling that she was going to be sick, or faint. Lowell told her to go and sit down. She thought it was nice of him and returned to the loft.

"Is he crying?" asked Candy.

What an odd question, Kate reflected.

"No, he's not. He doesn't seem a bit upset. Probably they weren't really friends, just business partners."

She wondered if Lowell ever felt anything besides anger and lust. It must have been those parents. A family of dead emotions. Bad enough for them, but even worse for her and Candy and Darren.

After a while he came back, his hands covered with earth. He brushed it off as best he could.

"Let's get in the car," he told her. "Get some food."

It was still morning and bright daylight. She was surprised at his recklessness, then remembered the switched license plates. Her head throbbed, but she thought the food might help.

The children hesitated, then followed. He did not try to stop them.

"I don't know if I can drive," she said. "I still feel dizzy."

108

"You better get yourself together, baby."

Would he call a person "baby" if he were going to kill her?

He would do anything he felt like doing. She was only a possession.

The children settled into the back seat. She heard Candy locking doors and helping Darren with his safety belt. She drove out of the barn, grateful that this time, at least, she could see the road.

At the end of the driveway, he told her to turn left.

"We didn't find anything—" she began.

"Do what I say. You want them looking for that license plate?"

Perhaps he was reconsidering his cleverness about the plates. She turned quickly onto the main road before anyone could spot a car in the driveway, and they traveled in the direction they had first gone last night. She hadn't seen it by day. Rolling mountains and isolated houses.

She didn't think to count the miles. She had no idea how long it was before they found a road that led down from the mountain. He told her to take it. Wherever there was a road, there would have to be civilization eventually.

And there was, after several more miles. Nearly at the foot of the mountain, they came to a very small village. It had only one commercial street, one small grocery store, and no fast-food restaurants.

"Park over there," said Lowell, "near that place where the flag is."

"I think that's a post office."

"I don't care what the hell it is, park in the back over there."

He ordered the children to sit on the floor with the blanket over their heads while he and Kate got out of the car.

"And don't make a move," he added. "You got that?

Keep the blanket on, and nobody moves, or I'll blow your heads off. Both of you."

Kate looked back as he led her across the street. Darren was only four. How could Lowell expect him to sit still and follow orders? To understand what would happen if he didn't?

As they entered the store, Lowell muttered, "Don't look at nobody, don't catch their eye. Here, take this." He handed her a shopping basket from a pile on the floor.

While she carried the basket, he filled it with bread, canned goods, soda. Anything that did not need refrigeration.

"Do we have a can opener?" she asked. "And matches?"

"We got Torrey's lighter."

"What about paper cups and plates?"

"What the hell you need that for?" But he humored her, sniffing in derision as he did so.

At the checkout counter he asked the clerk, "Any place around here where I can make a phone call?"

"There's a public phone over by the gas station."

On a rack next to the counter, Lowell found a *New York Times*, along with the *Boston Globe* and local papers.

"Got a *New York Post?*" he asked. *"Daily News?"*

"Only the *Times*," replied the storekeeper.

He bought a copy, and they went out to the car. The children, although half-suffocated under the blanket, had not moved.

He told Kate to drive to the gas station and park next to the phone booth, where he could watch them.

She saw him drop a coin into the telephone. Then more coins. She saw him talking. So he did know someone, somewhere. They would help to hide him, and then he wouldn't need her any more.

She opened a package of doughnuts and fed the children. Her hands felt oddly shaky, and she remembered about Torrey. It still did not seem real.

After a long conversation and more coins, he returned to the car.

She asked, "Is there anything else you want to do?"

"Like what?"

"I just wondered if maybe you'd want to get some more blankets."

"You see any blanket stores?"

She saw hardly any stores at all. Only auto parts and hardware. A card and toy shop, and a place for video rentals.

"Are we going back to the farm?"

"Where else?"

She did not know where else. She thought he might have planned a next step, something more permanent. It surprised her that he hadn't, and it bothered her to be near Torrey's body. Lowell seemed to think nothing of it.

"If you see any graveyards, let me know," he said.

"Grave . . . yards?" Did Torrey have to be in hallowed ground? She glanced at Lowell to see if he was serious.

"Graveyard," he said again, more loudly. "Do you know what's a graveyard?"

"Yes. Yes, I do."

"Then look for one."

"Do you want me to—to drive around and look?"

For them? Did he mean it for them? She could not imagine that he would care what sort of ground they were in.

"Just keep your eyes open," he said. "That's all. And let me know."

Chapter Fifteen

Ted went home to meet the detective.

"I probably won't be back," he told Elaine. "Unless something turns up right away." Meaning Kate, alive and well. And the children. They might be just down the street or on the next block. He would feel a little foolish, but it would be worth it.

The detective's name was Hennessy. He had blue eyes, iron-gray hair, and a pink face. He wondered why Ted had waited so long to call the police.

"I just didn't see how it could be necessary," Ted replied. He explained about the airport. He had assumed that Kate was waiting for him there. Detectives, he supposed, never assumed anything.

"That's right," said Hennessy. "It's one of the first things you learn. What about this morning?"

"Well, I thought—you see, I thought she might be staying with a friend. I figured I'd wait and see if she came home after she dropped the kids at school. But then I found my kids hadn't gotten to school. . . ."

The detective watched him with no expression at all.

"Well, I thought she had an engagement somewhere." He had explained it so many times to Elaine. "I couldn't remember what she said exactly, but I know she was going somewhere, and I thought, you know, maybe she decided to stay over."

Hennessy asked about the car.

Ted moistened his lips. "It's a Chevrolet station wagon. Full size. White. It's old. I forget the year. We bought it used." He was babbling, just the way Kate often did. This made him nervous. He did not know why.

"Plate number?"

"Uh . . ." He must know the plate number. He had seen it often enough. He felt more stupid than ever. "It would be on the insurance card, right?"

"No, it wouldn't."

"It would be on something. I must have it somewhere—in the den, where I keep all my stuff."

They went into the den. He had drawers full of papers. Things he meant to file someday, when he got around to buying a file cabinet. Hennessy said they could get the number from Motor Vehicles, but it would take a while, and in the case of missing persons, "a while" wasn't good enough.

Ted sorted through the papers while they talked. The mess embarrassed him further. "I'm really very orderly at the office," he said, "but there's so much to do around home. You know, maintenance work."

Hennessy knew. He had a home of his own.

"So you don't know if your family had any plans for the weekend."

"Only what my mother-in-law told me, that Kate was going to call her about a museum on Sunday. She never called. And as I said, I know there was something else, but I didn't pay much attention. I'm sort of a workaholic, and I—maybe that's what happened. She used to complain about it. Maybe she got fed up and just took off."

"She didn't leave a note?"

Kate would not have taken off without leaving a note.

He didn't think she would, anyway. No matter how fed up she might be, she was always fair.

"I just don't understand it," he said. "I don't understand what happened. If somebody got in the house and did anything—Wait, here it is."

He read the plate number. Hennessy wrote it down.

"It's kind of an old car," Ted said again. "It has some dents and scratches. The paint started flaking off, and we sprayed it. White paint is the worst, and we have a lot of salt air."

Babbling. Like Kate. He understood now why she talked so much. He had the feeling that he was trying to stave off something, a psychic assault of some kind.

Disapproval. That was it. Kate had a terror of disapproval. And because she worried about it, people tended to heap on more. Reluctantly, he included himself. Yes, he was guilty. Maybe she had had too much of that.

He still was sure she would have left a note.

"Do you find that you make people nervous?" he asked.

Hennessy looked up from the notebook in which he was writing.

"You're an authority figure," Ted explained. "I don't know why I feel this way. After all, I pay your salary. It's probably left over from childhood. I have to tell you, this whole thing makes me nervous as hell."

"Why does it make you nervous?" Hennessy asked with interest.

"Well, in the first place, it seems kind of incompetent to misplace one's family. And in the second place, I can't help thinking that you might wonder if I had something to do with it." He hoped, by his frankness, to make the whole idea seem absurd. Or maybe it would have the opposite effect.

Hennessy showed no reaction. "Did you?"

"Of course not. I wasn't even here."

"We don't know when they disappeared," Hennessy said.

"That's true." Had he been right to think they might suspect him? Or had he just put a lousy idea into this guy's head?

"I wouldn't have any reason," he pointed out.

Would they find out about Elaine? Couldn't they understand it was just a weekend thing?

"Can you tell me what they might have been wearing?" asked the detective.

"No, unless it happened Friday. I mean, if they disappeared Friday." Ted rubbed his chin. He couldn't even remember what they had been wearing on Friday, when he last saw them.

"I didn't make a note of it. I didn't think it would—be important."

"Mm hm," said Hennessy, scribbling.

"It doesn't look as if they packed anything, though," Ted went on. "I checked. I mean, you know, you can't remember everything a person owns, but there was an awful lot there. I didn't notice any, you know, gaps."

He went on to report what Doris Ackerman had seen.

"I don't know if she actually saw them in the car—I don't know if you could from there—but she saw the car going out."

"Any idea where they might have been going on a rainy day?"

"It was raining?"

"Torrents."

"That's right. Doris said—" How could he have forgotten? "Oh, hey, that's it!"

"What's it?" asked Hennessy.

"A barbecue! I knew there was someplace she said she was going. And I told her it was supposed to rain, so they must have put it off until Sunday—"

"Hold it, hold it. You're saying she went to a barbecue

115

on Sunday, that was supposed to be held Saturday—"

"But it rained!"

"And she still isn't back by noon on Monday, and the kids aren't in school?"

"Uh . . . yeah." He felt like a balloon losing its air. "You're right. Oh, hell."

"We have to consider everything, of course," Hennessy assured him. "Do you know where this barbecue was going to be held?"

"No, I don't. I didn't ask her. I, uh, had my mind on the trip."

"Okay. Did she have any errands that you know of for the weekend?"

"No, she did her shopping Friday."

"Doctor appointments?"

"None that I know of, unless there was an emergency. Hell, I didn't check the hospital."

"Don't you think she might have called you?"

"Right. Yes, if one of the kids was sick, she would have called me in Chicago."

"Any birthday parties?"

"Wait. I didn't think. Just a second." Ted went out to the kitchen and returned with the wall calendar. Flowers. That was the picture for May. A formal garden somewhere.

"All it says is 'Ted Chicago.' "

"Let me see." Hennessy took the calendar. "Ted Chicago p.m." was down for Friday. Above it, Kate had written "Suit." She had "Ted Chic." for Saturday, and on Sunday, "Ted ret. p.m."

"Mm hm," he said.

Ted rubbed his chin and tried to be objective. The notes made her seem so alive. So very much present.

"I don't understand it," he said.

"You don't understand what this means?"

116

"I don't understand the whole thing. It's just—crazy. I did tell you I talked to her mother, didn't I?"

"Yes, you did. Do you think your neighbor might be home? The one who saw the car?"

"Probably. That's where she usually is." Everybody was in the right place except Kate.

Assuring him that he would stay in touch, Hennessy walked through a gap in the hedge to the Ackerman house.

Ted paced the floor. He ought to go back to the office, but didn't think he could face it. On the other hand, staying at home and stewing was a real downer.

It wasn't long before he saw the detective leave Doris's house, get into his car and drive away.

"No leads." That was how the media would put it. "The police are still looking for leads."

He wondered if it would be on the radio. In the newspaper. He hoped not. He hated the idea of publicity.

Still, the more people who knew about it, the greater the chance of something turning up. Or even Kate and the children turning up. If she was hanging out with a boyfriend, for instance, the publicity might embarrass her just enough.

Or embarrass her into running still further away. Disappearing for good.

He tried to imagine spending his whole life never knowing what had happened to his family. Coming home at the end of each day to an empty house. Always wondering.

My God, he thought, *some people really have to deal with that. Especially when it's kids, lost kids.*

How did they endure it? And if they couldn't, which he didn't see how they could, what did they do?

Chapter Sixteen

A cold wind blew across the Heavenly Rest Cemetery.

Kate looked up at the sky. It was heavy and gray, with no break in the clouds. They had been out since five o'clock that morning in the raw cold. She had hoped the sun would warm them, but there was no sun that day.

"Mommy," said Candy, "I'm freezing."

"We all are," Kate replied. She worried about Darren, who had developed a cough.

Lowell called over to them, "Keep looking."

It was the second cemetery they had visited, trying to find someone who had died as an infant at about the time Lowell was born. He had insisted that they go out early, when no one was around to bother them.

She thought it was because of the telephone call yesterday. He would not discuss it, but she had the impression that he had been asking for help and hadn't gotten it. Now he was on his own.

"I have to get a new identity," was all he told her. "First I get a phony birth certificate. If I have that, I can get Social Security. The works."

"How can you?" she had asked. "Wouldn't they have a record that the person died?"

"Nah. They don't match up birth and death records. I

just take that person's name and apply for a birth certificate. A duplicate. I tell them I lost mine."

"It sounds horrible," she said, "passing yourself off as—as a dead—a perfectly innocent baby—who died."

"Shit. What do you care?"

"And what if you go and apply for your birth certificate in a small place like this, and they happen to know who the baby was? What if they know the family?"

"You don't know what you're talking about," he sneered.

Probably he had it all worked out. She shouldn't have questioned him.

Shouldn't have forewarned him. He might have gotten caught that way.

Candy said, "Mommy, I felt a drop."

Then Kate felt one, too. And another. "Lowell?"

He was too far away to hear her.

"You kids get in the car," she told them.

Candy looked stricken. "What if he doesn't let us?"

"I'll deal with him. Just get in the car, especially Darren, with that cold."

The children started ahead of her. She wished they would run, but they didn't, as the rain began to fall harder. Lowell, oblivious to the weather, continued his search.

For three hours they had been trudging through graveyards. "It's no use," she had tried to tell him when they couldn't find anything at the first one. "Most babies just don't die anymore. It's a real long shot that you'll ever find what you're looking for."

He hadn't wanted to believe her. This was his only chance, she supposed. And he told her other people had gotten away with it.

A few yards to the right, she noticed a small headstone. A small one often meant it was the grave of a child. How could they have missed it?

The child's name was Lesley and it had been born in 1950. Too long ago. Much too long ago. Besides, she couldn't tell whether Lesley was a boy or a girl.

Still, it was the best possibility yet. In fact, so far, the only one.

"Lowell!"

He had stopped the children and was waving his gun at them. She ran to explain.

"I told them to get in the car. It's starting to rain, and Darren's getting a cold, and he can't read anyway. And—"

She would not tell him about the stone she had seen. He would probably reject it. He would say it was a girl's name and too old. Besides, she owed him nothing.

"Couldn't they get in the car?" she asked. "I'll stay and help you."

"Aaah, let's go. It's getting late." He sounded disappointed.

Darren sniffled and then sneezed. She reached into her pocket for a tissue. Her last one. She hoped Lowell would want to go shopping again. She began to feel guilty, thinking of the gravestone. It wasn't fair not to tell him.

She reminded herself that he wasn't being fair to her. None of this was fair.

But he had fed them. All along, he had fed and looked after them. And despite his threats, he hadn't killed them . . . yet. . . .

Sheltering Darren under her jacket, she hurried on toward the car. A little way ahead, Lowell waited for her. When she caught up with him, he held something out to her.

A yellow rose, its petals wilting and faded.

"Where did you get that?" she asked.

He nodded back toward a row of graves. A drying bouquet lay on one of them. She thought the rose must have been its centerpiece. Someone had meant it for a person they loved, and she had no right—

But Lowell had meant it for her. She looked up at his face, at his hard, unreadable eyes, and she was strangely touched.

"Thank you," she said as she took the rose. Then they all walked on toward the car.

Ted felt suspended in a world without time. It was already Tuesday morning. His family was gone. Vanished. And he was afraid.

He hadn't slept well that night. He kept listening to the neighborhood sounds. It was odd that the neighborhood should make its usual sounds when everything was so different.

He had gotten up early, brewed his coffee and looked at the newspaper and the television. He found them both annoyingly cosmic. World events seemed petty to him now.

He turned on the kitchen radio to the local station. The big news was a threatened railroad strike. He didn't give a damn about a railroad strike. He didn't want to hear about any bodies being found, either, but guessed he'd rather know than spend his life not knowing.

At ten minutes to nine, since the boss was always there early, he telephoned his office.

He didn't ask for a leave of absence. He simply told them he was taking it. He said he knew they would understand.

After allowing a few more minutes for the attendance records to be processed, he called Mrs. Wong.

"No, she's still out," Mrs. Wong replied. "You haven't heard anything yet?"

"Not a word. But I did call the police. They said they'd put out a bulletin. I don't know what else they're doing."

He couldn't wait for the police. He would have to do it himself. Just get out there and look for them. It was all he could think of.

He got into his car and began to drive around Belle Harbor. He needed a game plan, but he hadn't any. He supposed the police knew better how to go about this— but were they doing it?

He found himself passing the school. He stopped for a moment and contemplated the red-brick facade, the long windows decorated with paper cutouts of flowers and birds and rabbits.

That's where Candy should be now, he thought, feeling a squeeze in his chest as he remembered the rabbits she had drawn for Easter. And the big purple one her grandmother had given her. She loved that purple bunny.

And Darren. Little Darren, who was scarcely more than an infant. If Kate had run off and taken the children, she was in for a lot of trouble. They were his, too.

But he didn't think Kate had done that.

He drove on, wondering if he should go into the school and talk to somebody. Candy's teacher, or some of the children. Candy might have said something. Dropped a hint or two.

He would leave that for the police. They knew how to ask the right questions.

He passed the supermarket. Kate had been there Friday. She had stopped at the cleaner's to pick up his suit. Might she have said anything to the cleaner? She did talk a lot.

He wasn't being very effective. Hennessy would have known what to do. But Hennessy probably had ten other cases going at the same time.

He pulled over to the curb, next to a parking meter, and tried to think. Where would a woman take two young children on a rainy Saturday in May, while Daddy was away on a business trip?

Not to the beach. They might have done that if it had been a nice day.

She usually wrote birthday parties on the calendar.

Her mother hadn't seen her. Could she have visited a friend? In the pouring rain? How about shopping? Maybe the kids needed socks, or shoes, or jeans.

But in the rain? Wouldn't she wait till it cleared a little?

He thought it must have been Saturday, since she had promised to call her mother on Sunday and hadn't done it. Kate didn't share her mother's passion for museums but wouldn't have let her down. She'd at least have called. It was too bad Jeanette hadn't tried to reach her when she didn't hear anything. At least they would know whether Kate had or hadn't been home on Sunday morning.

He thought of the movies. She might take them there. He drove to the town's one theater and found they were showing something that looked like a horror picture. Scratch that. Kate would never let small kids see a horror picture. He started his car and began to cruise again.

But where? It was stupid, just driving around. As if he might, by some chance, spot her car. Or her.

Saltport? Could she possibly have gone to check on Elaine's apartment, thinking he might be there instead of Chicago, and then met with some difficulty?

It seemed unlikely that she would have done such a thing. She wasn't jealous of Elaine. Only of his job.

Still, he couldn't seem to come up with anything better. He might get ideas from something he happened to see. And so he went to Saltport.

He avoided Hyland. He didn't want them to think he was being frivolous. He drove past Elaine's building and wished there were a doorman he could ask, but there wasn't.

He drove along South Street, the older shopping area.

She never went there. She preferred the mall, where everything was new and seductive. She said she liked having all the stores together. And you could go to the mall in the rain.

He drove to the mall.

It surprised him to find the parking lot almost full in the middle of a weekday morning. Who was it full of? A lot of the cars, he supposed, belonged to employees.

He began at Sears, Roebuck and worked his way down to Food World at the other end, looking for special sales or anything that might have inspired her to come out in the rain.

There was a sale in the jeans outlet, but they didn't have children's sizes. He tried two shoe stores, and then returned to Sears.

The trouble with the mall, he decided, was the impersonality of it. It wasn't like your neighborhood shops where the salespeople knew their regular customers by sight and often by name. He couldn't very well ask, "Did a woman and two children come in here Saturday?"

Sure, several hundred of them. What did you have in mind?

Besides, a lot of these stores hired teenage help for weekends only, and the kids were not there now.

He stood in the middle of Sears's children's department and groaned. A guy like Hennessy could have found the right people to ask. He had the resources and the clout. But it wasn't Ted's place to tell Hennessy his business and suggest that he try the mall, since there was no particular reason to think they had been here, any more than some other place.

He had run out of ideas. Completely. There was nothing to do now but return to his car and go home.

Chapter Seventeen

The yellow rose lay on the seat between them. One yellow rose. It was the best he could do. She felt torn, almost sorry for him, but hated him all the more.

Hate and revulsion. That was what she felt.

She watched for the road into the farm. It was raining steadily now. A cold rain, not warm, as it had been on the day—*that* day.

"Tomorrow morning," said Lowell, "we'll go out again. Maybe tonight, if it quits raining."

She asked, "Isn't there any other way? Any other place you can look?"

"What place?"

"I guess not. I was thinking of old newspapers, but you'd have to go to a library. And they might not put in about a baby's death."

"Watch it!"

She braked quickly. It was their road. She had almost missed it again.

Candy opened her window and prepared to reach out quickly. The small trees grew so close together that they almost touched the car. She wondered if she might do better to wait until another time. The feathers would not show up so well if they were wet. The bright pink feathers on her key ring. But there were so few chances.

Darren began to cough.

Not now, Darren!

In the front seat, Lowell put a hand to the back of his neck. "What's that cold? You got a window open?"

She closed it quickly. Her stomach churned with a horrible feeling, dizzy and sick, as if something were about to happen. Something terrible. To her.

Lowell looked around. Her hand tightened over the key ring. She hadn't had a chance . . .

"I felt sick," she explained, as he watched her through slitty eyes.

Hadn't had a chance to put it out. It didn't work. Nothing worked.

"You're getting *sick*?"

"It's okay now." She sat frozen, twisted, clutching the feathers. He hated her. And what if he saw the key ring?

"We're almost there," said her mother. "Almost." The bumping of the car on that road began to make the sickness real.

He was going to kill her. She knew it. Her and Darren. He hated kids. Every time they had to eat, he fussed about the money.

But he needed their mother. He needed her to drive the car. It was the first time Candy had ever seen a man who couldn't drive.

Kate drove into the barn and turned off the engine. She wished they could stay in the car. It was warmer than the rest of the barn.

But Lowell flung open his door and pulled Candy from the back seat.

"You're sick, you get out of here before you throw up."

"I'm okay now," Candy squeaked. Her terror was a knife in Kate's heart. Her face had paled, whether from sickness or fear Kate could not tell.

126

Candy got out of the car and stood shivering. She held her hand in a fist, which she gradually moved toward the pocket of her jeans, all the time staring at Lowell like a rabbit at the end of a gun.

Darren started another coughing fit, distracting Lowell and making Candy jerk guiltily, to clasp both hands as though in prayer.

Darren gasped for breath and coughed again. His face turned a deep red.

Lowell shouted, "Can't you stop that?"

Darren, coughing and unable to speak, looked back at him with watery eyes.

Kate scooped him up and carried him outside. The rain fell on them both, but it was the only place where she could get him away from Lowell.

Candy followed her outside. They stood under a tree. Kate hoped there wouldn't be lightning.

"We shouldn't stay here," she said. "We have no dry clothes to change into."

"His cold is going to get worse," said Candy.

"What have you got in your hand?"

Candy hesitated, then reluctantly uncurled her fingers. Kate caught a glimpse of the pink key ring, its feathers crushed from being held so tightly.

"I'd forgotten you had that," she said. "Why are you holding it that way? What were you doing?"

"I was going to put it on a branch when we came in this road, so somebody'd see it, and they wouldn't know why it was there, and maybe they'd come in and look, but when I opened the window—"

"Oh, Candy."

"What?"

"Honey, please don't—don't do anything to make him mad."

"But, Mommy . . ."

"You don't understand, honey. He's dangerous." Kate

looked around quickly to be sure he was out of earshot.

Candy collapsed against her and began to cry. "I want to get away from here."

"We all do. Oh, darling, I love you both so much. I'll think of something, I will."

Darren's coughing had subsided. As she led them back to the barn, she added, "I'm not sure anybody'd notice a thing like that, anyway. It's very small, and cars drive by so fast."

Candy nodded, slipping the key ring into her pocket.

Kate helped Darren into the back of the car and covered him with the blanket. It was the best place for him, but Lowell sat in the front seat, cleaning his gun.

"Stay quiet, Darren. Try to go to sleep. You need a lot of rest to get over a cold."

But lying down made the coughing begin again. Violent spasms shook the car. Lowell snapped his gun together and jumped from the front seat.

"Cut that out!" he roared, elbowing past her.

"Please!" she begged. "He can't help it."

Lowell dragged the child from the car and pulled him toward the stairs.

"What are you doing?" Kate screamed. She tried to pry his hand from Darren's arm. "He can't help it! He's got a cold, and it's your fault. I'm telling you, Lowell, if you hurt my kids—"

He sneered, close to her face. "What are *you* going to do, huh?"

She stared at him, unflinching. She would kill him, tear him apart with her bare hands, if he hurt her children.

He laughed and went on up the stairs. Darren, coughing and crying. Darren's little arm in his grip. She followed, clawing. She caught a flash of pink. It was Candy, right on her heels.

He started toward the loft door. She aimed her thumb

at his eyeball. He caught her arm and twisted it. She kicked at his legs. Wearing sneakers. Damn sneakers. He flung her away and she fell.

Candy flew at him. He pulled Darren toward the hole in the floor.

Not Candy, too!

She hurled herself at Lowell, clawing again. She was like a cat attacking a mountain. *Damn, damn, why do I have to be so weak?*

The floor gaped.

"No, no, no!" she screamed.

Again she threw herself, seizing Darren in her arms. She clutched at him, wrestling for him.

She slipped. Her foot went over the edge. *I'm going to die, and who will help them?*

He pulled her back and flung her away. She rolled over, reaching.

Reaching—for empty air.

And Candy. Screaming.

Candy's screams went on and on.

Chapter Eighteen

Ted shook his head. There must have been something wrong with him. He couldn't remember, couldn't think.

She *had* said something about that weekend, something besides the barbecue. What in hell was it? Again he damned himself for not having listened—but how could he have known?

He took his place in a line of cars waiting to leave the parking lot. Through the ticking of his directional signal, he groped for something. Vital. More recent than Friday, when he had last talked to her. It was something that had just happened. Something—

A torn poster on the lamppost near where he had parked his car. Balloons, and a clown's smiling face. A red-haired clown. Ronald McDonald, he had thought, but he remembered the date. It was Saturday. He knew that much.

"Hey," he said. The light changed. The cars began to move.

He hesitated, then flipped his signal lever. The car behind him blew its horn.

He drove back to where he had been parked. Another car was already in the space. He stopped behind it and got out to look at the poster.

Whatever it was, it had taken place here. Right here at

the mall. On Saturday. He saw the letters CIR. The rest was torn off. Below, in smaller letters, there were fragments of words: Clo— Fun!

He still couldn't remember what she had said, but something clicked. This was the kind of thing you would take your kids to on a rainy weekend. Maybe. Unless you hated driving in the rain. But if the kids knew about it, they would badger her. They were good at that.

He drove around, looking for another place to park. Maybe he was wrong, but it was the best thing he had come up with so far. In fact, the only thing.

Somebody was pulling out. He beat a Renault into the space and ignored its squawk of outrage. He was beyond playing by the rules.

He headed back to Sears. Past the tool section was a winding corridor, where several times he had taken Darren to the men's room. There were pay phones there, but he didn't know Hennessy's number.

He had to ask directory assistance. Finally he found his way through to the right office. They informed him that Hennessy was out.

"Oh, hell," he said and left a message. He told them where he was, but knew Hennessy would never find him in the mall. Still, maybe something would get across to the good detective.

He left the corridor and went back to the tool department. The salesman was busy selling paint. He passed through housewares and small appliances. They were all busy.

Office supplies. That was no good. Children's clothing. The best bet so far. A woman with two preschoolers was looking at swimsuits. While she fingered something in red with white dots, he inserted himself between her and the sales clerk, who pointedly ignored him because it was not his turn.

"Excuse me," he said, "this is very important. I'm investigating a missing-persons case. Can you tell me anything about what happened here Saturday?"

"What do you mean?" asked the clerk.

"That thing with the clowns and balloons."

"Circus Day?"

"Is that what it was?" He thought of the CIR.

"What do you want to know about it?"

"I want to know what sort of thing it was. And where. What were the hours?"

"Excuse me, sir, I have a customer."

"I'll wait."

He waited. The customer couldn't make up her mind. He had no sympathy with that. A child's swimsuit was not a lifetime commitment. What did it matter which one she chose?

One of the toddlers began to complain. It was getting near lunchtime. He blessed the child's appetite and finally had the saleslady to himself.

"You're investigating something?" she asked.

"Yes. A woman and two children disappeared last Saturday."

"Are you a cop?"

He wished he were. He decided to level with her.

"I'm working with the police," he said. "They can't be everywhere at once. I'm the woman's husband. The children's father. I was away on a business trip when it happened. I saw a poster about Saturday and have reason to believe they might have come here if it was a big event."

She was a small, dark-eyed woman. Smaller than Kate and not as pretty. He couldn't tell whether she believed what he said, but it didn't matter, as long as she talked to him.

"It was the whole mall," she said. "It was . . . I don't know, mostly clowns. And a trained seal."

"The whole mall? So it was a pretty big thing? Was it crowded?"

"Are you kidding?"

Crowded with women and small children. His family would have stood out like three grains of sand on a beach. And he didn't even know what they were wearing.

"Thanks," he said. "It's a start, anyway."

"Are they really missing? Since *Saturday*? I didn't see anything in the paper."

"You will, I'm sure."

Maybe that was what they needed. Exposure. Maybe he should go to the Saltport *Herald*.

Or maybe he should consult with Hennessy first.

Chapter Nineteen

She lay in the car, holding Darren, and remembered all the things she had heard about criminals.

Power. That was what he wanted. She mustn't threaten it.

And she had. She had threatened him.

But what could I do?

Candy crawled in beside her. "My neck," she whimpered. "He hurt my neck."

"I know, baby. I'll think of something."

There had to be a way. They were three to his one.

But two of them were children, and she was only Kate. Her physical strength was no match for his. It had been maddening that she couldn't even dent him.

Because of that, her threats were empty. Besides, *he* wanted to do the bullying. He was a small punk, an inadequate peanut, and this was his chance to kick someone around.

I've got to be smarter than he is, she thought. *It's the only thing I have.*

And I can drive a car.

"He was going to push Darren through that hole," Candy said.

"I don't know if he really was. He might have been only teasing."

She said it for the children. Even for herself. She did not want to believe he could have been serious.

"But, Mommy, that's not fun teasing."

"No, it's not. It's a power trip. He seems to need it. That's what bullying is. Bullies are people who don't feel good about themselves."

"But I don't like it."

"Nobody likes it. It's not a genuine achievement, so they have to go on bullying because they still don't feel good about themselves."

Psychology shit. That was what he would have called it. Was she making excuses for him, as he did for himself?

No, she thought, she was only trying to understand him. Know thine enemy. It was very important.

She didn't want to know him, after what he had done to her children. She wanted to strangle him, to kick and stomp him. But that, apparently, was not to be.

"We'll have to try to get along with him," she said, "until we can find a way out of here. I know Darren can't help coughing, but let's just try not to upset him, okay?"

"How are we going to find a way out of here?" Candy asked desolately.

"We will." She had to say it.

She lifted the blanket that covered Darren and, for the second time, gently probed his arm and shoulder to be sure nothing was broken. Darren had been mauled and badly shocked, but he was alive.

Maybe she had saved his life after all. Lowell had such a foul, impulsive temper, she was quite sure he really had intended to kill her boy. Maybe, by blocking him, she had caused enough delay to make him change his mind.

But next time . . . what would happen next time?

135

Chapter Twenty

"I've been trying to get hold of you," Hennessy said. "Where the hell are you?"

"You're even harder to get hold of," Ted replied from his phone booth at Sears. "Didn't you get my message? I'm at the Brookside Mall."

"I got your message, all right. What the hell are you doing at the mall?"

"Looking for my family. I think they might have been coming here when Doris Ackerman saw them drive out Saturday."

"Hold it, hold it. I have some news for you. They found the car."

"Found—the car?" He battled a torrent of mixed feelings. They found the car. That was progress. They found the car without his family. That was ominous. "Where? Uh—where?"

"In Boston. That's what I don't quite figure. It's in a parking lot at Logan Airport."

"Airport? In Boston?"

"Yeah, well, that's why I tried to get hold of you. The plate number checks out. I'm not too sure about the color. It's a tan station wagon."

"But hers is white."

"Dead white?"

He didn't like the word *dead*.

"Well, sort of off-white. Maybe a little dingy. Maybe it could be mistaken for tan."

"I wish you were home," said Hennessy. "I want you to look up something for me. The insurance stuff or the title certificate. You don't keep that with the car, I hope."

"No, no, I have it. I could go home right now."

"I'll meet you there."

Dear God, thought Ted as he went out to his car. A tan station wagon. How could that happen? Somebody stole it and painted it? His family was dead.

Maybe it was covered with dust or mud. That had to be it. But why Boston?

When he arrived at home, Hennessy's car was already there. So was another car, a small red sports model, parked out on the road. He recognized Hennessy in the crowd by the front walk, along with two other men and a woman. His home was no longer his castle, it was a mob scene.

The woman and one of the men rushed to meet him. The woman had reddish hair, sharp brown eyes, and brown slacks. Her companion was tall and young. Dark hair. It was all he noticed.

"We're from the Saltport *Herald*," said the woman. "I'm Sandra Geis. This is Potter."

"Boyd Potter." The young man grinned. His hand jerked forward tentatively and then withdrew. He was inexperienced. Didn't know how to behave like a reporter.

Geis had already pulled out a notebook. "Mr. Armstrong, can you tell us how you first found out your family was gone?"

137

"Uh . . ." He looked at Hennessy.

"Let's get the car thing settled first," said Hennessy and introduced the second man, a darkly handsome detective named Rizzo.

Ted didn't know if he wanted the reporters in his house. "How did *you* find out?" he asked them.

"I have a nose for news," Geis replied.

"Do you mind staying outside? This is a private home."

Geis scowled. She probably wanted to comb the whole house. He looked to see if she had a camera.

Potter had one. He supposed they would take pictures of the outside. People would come to gape and trample his lawn. He unlocked the door and admitted the two detectives, then quickly closed it.

"What did you tell them?" he asked.

"Nothing," said Hennessy.

"I was debating whether it might help to bring in the media. But this is kind of sudden and overwhelming."

"It always is."

Ted and Hennessy went into the den while Rizzo looked around the rest of the house.

"Anything that has the vehicle ID on it," Hennessy said. Ted found that the vehicle identification was on more things than the plate number was. He produced an insurance card. The detective compared it with something he had written down.

"It doesn't check. It's not the same car."

"I don't understand."

"It's not your wife's car. The ID doesn't check."

"But the license?"

"You ever take the plates off a car? It's not so hard to do, is it? Somebody switched the plates."

"It's very hard to do. The bolts always get corroded." He was just talking. Denying the obvious. He dropped his head into his hand.

138

Hennessy's voice came through a roaring in his ears. "We'll keep looking for it, of course."

"How, without the plates?"

"It'll take a while, but we'll find out what plate number's supposed to be on that tan car. Now, do you want to tell me about the mall?"

It seemed ridiculous now as he described what he had been doing there. Circus Day. An innocent circus day. He knew they were dead.

"If that's where they went," he said, "I can see maybe somebody stealing the car out of the parking lot, but where's my family? Why weren't they in the mall? Why didn't they just come out and find the car gone, and take a taxi home? I don't understand."

With surprising gentleness, Hennessy said, "We don't know what happened. Don't jump to conclusions. We'll find out. I think what you'd better do now is give me some pictures of them. You've got pictures, right?"

There were three family albums and an envelope of snapshots not yet pasted in. As Ted went through them, he noticed that his fingertips were numb. His head was numb, too.

Somehow the two reporters had gotten into the house. They clamored for their own set of pictures.

"Did you get any calls?" asked Geis, elbowing her way past the detectives.

"Calls?"

"Ransom demands? Anything like that?"

"No, nothing. We—we don't have money." He would still talk of "we," even though he might be the only one left.

"Sometimes it's a matter of opportunity." Geis seemed to be all over him. He felt surrounded by her. "You never know how you might look to somebody else."

He couldn't look rich to anybody, when he wasn't.

They should have asked to see his tax return before they took his family.

He heard the young man say, "Probably somebody just wanted the car."

And Geis snapped, "Shut up, Potter."

Ted was aware of her bending over him with that infernal notebook. He couldn't see how she did it, until he realized that he was sitting down.

She asked, "Why don't you go on television? You know, have them tape it for the evening news. You'd ask for any information about your family. Maybe cry a little."

"I'm afraid that's not my style," Ted replied.

"It could help."

The young man was busy with his own theory. "You know, it really might have been somebody who needed to get somewhere and didn't have a car. Remember that bank robbery?"

"Shut *up*, Potter."

"Nobody ever found those guys, did they?"

"Not yet," said Hennessy's voice from the foot of the stairs. Ted hadn't known he was still in the house. He felt as though his mind had pieces missing from it, like a puzzle.

"They could have come here." Potter went to the back window and looked out. "You have a garden shed. They could have hidden there for a while."

"It's locked," said Ted.

"Yeah, right." Potter saw the big padlock. "Any basement windows?"

"They're locked. And they have permanent screens."

"Nothing's been tampered with." Hennessy nodded his partner toward the door. "I'll be in touch."

"I think they should check it out," said Potter.

"You're an idiot," said Geis.

In the kitchen, the telephone rang.

140

He wanted to answer it. He wanted it to be Kate. He was afraid.

"Would you please leave?" he asked the reporters.

Geis shouldered her handbag and followed him out to the kitchen.

He picked up the phone. *Kate. Please be Kate.*

"Oh—hi, Elaine. No, nothing."

"Some detective was trying to find you," said Elaine. "They called you at work. They had the car."

"No, they didn't. They had the license plates. It was another car."

"Oh, Ted."

So it didn't sound good to her, either.

"I was over at the mall," he said. "I thought that's where they might have gone. There was some sort of shindig on Saturday, for kids."

"But what could have happened at a shindig for kids?"

Maybe the Potter fellow was right, and someone had been lurking. But what did they do with his family?

There wasn't any blood around the house. They must have been taken alive.

But they were dead now. He knew it. Somewhere between here and Boston. It was a lot of ground to cover.

"Keep me posted," said Elaine.

"Right."

He had forgotten about Geis. Another of those blanks in his head.

"Who's Elaine?" she asked.

"Somebody I work with."

"She keeps in close touch with you?"

"Of course. I work with her. I took the day off—"

"She didn't have anything to do with that business trip you were on, did she?"

He stared at her, damning reporters. He felt his face change color.

"Never mind," she told him sweetly.

Never mind what? He couldn't believe she was letting him off so easily.

"Listen, Miss Geis—"

"Just call me Sandra. Here's my card. I'll be talking to you, Armstrong."

He didn't want her card. He watched her go out and get into her car, watched Potter back onto his lawn to turn around.

He wondered if he ought to call Elaine and warn her. He thought she could probably handle it better than he could.

He went down to the basement to see whether anyone might have gotten in. He found all the screens intact, all the windowsills coated with their usual dirt and grime.

There was no way he could tell about the garage. She might have left it unlocked, but he didn't really think she would be so absentminded. It had been locked when he came home. He could not imagine kidnappers, killers, or thieves taking the trouble to do that.

No, he thought, the house was untouched. It—whatever it was—had to have happened somewhere else.

Boyd Potter drove down Elton Avenue, slowing the car when they passed the Ocean Bank. He tried to pick up vibes. You could learn a lot from vibes, but that was something he never discussed with Sandra.

"Get moving," she said.

"Where to?"

"Hyland Aircraft. There's a woman angle."

"What do you mean?"

"Don't be dumb, Potts. He has a girlfriend. That puts a whole new light on this thing."

"Why? You don't think he did anything?"

"I didn't say that, and I'm not going to."

He hated her smug grin.

"You need a pass to get in there," he said.

"Only parts of it. We're not going to those parts. Drive faster, will you?"

He shook his head and drove faster. He couldn't believe the guy would do anything like that. Play around, maybe, but nothing drastic. It wasn't in his vibes.

He didn't think Sandra believed it, either.

Hennessy and Rizzo parked their car by Sears and went in through the hardware entrance.

"It's a thought," Hennessy had said. "He knows his family."

Until they heard from the Boston police, who were tracing the true identity of the tan station wagon, they hadn't much else to work with.

"My wife was here on Saturday," said Rizzo as they walked through the store. "Nobody's going to remember one particular woman and two kids."

"We've got pictures, right?"

"I'm telling you."

They divided up the pictures. Rizzo had two, one of the wife and one of the kids posing with their Easter baskets. Hennessy had a snap of all three on the living-room sofa. It was overexposed, and the little girl was grinning madly, showing off her missing front teeth.

They asked a cashier, who shook her head.

They asked a woman in the children's clothing department.

"Is that them?" The woman seized Hennessy's picture and studied it closely. "There was a man in here a little while ago asking about some missing people."

"Yeah, we know. You didn't see these people on Saturday?"

"Mister, you couldn't have found your own mother in this place."

"I told you," said Rizzo.

They went out into the mall. Hennessy said, "You go down the left side and I'll take the right." It was a needle in a haystack, and maybe the people hadn't been here at all, but it had to be done.

His first stop was a small department store. He skipped the cosmetics and the gourmet foods, which were right by the door, and went upstairs to the toy department. Back on the main floor, he tried children's clothing.

His next stop was a jeans outlet. They didn't carry kids' sizes, but he asked anyway. As he left, he saw Rizzo entering the Fanny Farmer candy shop.

A discount pharmacy and then another department store. B. Dalton books and Radio Shack. A card shop. A record store. A place that specialized in waterbeds. As he entered Woolworth's, he saw Rizzo coming out of a hosiery shop and going into a drugstore. In another few minutes they'd reach the supermarket, and that would be the end of it.

The Woolworth's cashier wore her glasses on a chain. She adjusted them and examined the picture.

"I wasn't here Saturday, but I think I've seen that woman. A lot of people come in here, you know."

"I'm aware of that," said Hennessy. "It's just a chance."

"What did she do?"

"Nothing, as far as I know. We're looking for her, is all."

A loud whistle made him turn his head. He wished Rizzo wouldn't whistle.

"Thanks for your help, miss." He went out to the mall where Rizzo stood with his fingers in his mouth, ready to let loose again.

"I am not a dog," Hennessy told him, "and I'm not a taxi."

"Come in here." Rizzo led him toward the drugstore. "We just might have something."

The pictures were spread out on the counter, and the druggist was examining them.

"I'm sure these are the people," he said. "She was getting a headache and she came in here for aspirin. I gave her a glass of water."

"That was Saturday?" asked Rizzo. "Are you sure?"

"I'm sure. I remember all that circus hullabaloo. The little girl had a paper hat. They were giving those out, I think."

"Was anybody with them?"

"No, they came in by themselves, just the three of them. The lady wanted aspirin. I made some remark about how come she felt bad when all that gala stuff was going on. I like to talk to my customers, you know? They're each of them people, not just customers. I like people. The little girl said something about her father being away and mommy missed him. I can't remember. I gave them some little things I had. The lady seemed so down, I gave her a perfume sample. I gave the kids . . . I can't remember. Some junky stuff I had around."

When he paused for breath, Hennessy asked, "Do you remember what time that was?"

"Gee." The man scratched his head. "I don't know. Three. Three-thirty, maybe. It could have been earlier. I don't watch the clock."

"What were they wearing?"

"Oh, now that's a tough one. What happened, anyway? What's the problem?"

Hennessy told him what the problem was. The man appeared shocked. He took another look at the pictures, then closed his eyes.

145

"Let's see. The little girl . . . I remember her. She had the hat. It was pink. It must have matched her jacket. I remember a lot of pink. And blue. The boy had a blue jacket. Shiny. One of those sports things."

"What kind of blue?"

"Medium. Bright. The mother? Brown eyes. I remember her eyes. And maybe a brown jacket. What do you think happened?"

"We have no idea," Hennessy answered, "but this is a start. Can you describe the paper hat?"

"Sure, I guess so. It fit over her head"—he demonstrated with his hands—"and had a sort of brim, like those knit things ladies wear. And a big flower on the side, a paper flower."

"Which side?"

"Uh—right. I mean right as you faced her. It would be her left."

"Can you draw me a picture of it?" Hennessy handed over his notebook and pencil.

"Of the hat? Uh—sure. I'm not too good at drawing."

He wasn't. He erased a lot. Hennessy was glad he had a good eraser on the pencil. Usually he didn't.

The druggist went on talking while he sketched.

"I saw a couple of other kids with hats like that, in different colors. It was a rainy day, see. They wouldn't have worn them outside, so I guess somebody must have been passing them out. Or making them. It was a kind you can make, you know, twisting paper into a shape."

"You've been a great help, mister."

"If there's anything else . . ."

"What direction did they go when they left here?"

"That way. Toward Sears."

"Was anybody with them? Anybody seem to be following them? Watching them?"

"I didn't happen to notice. It was just a glimpse I had of them turning that way. Let me know, will you?"

146

"Sure will."

As they left the store, Rizzo asked, "Now what?"

"Now," said Hennessy, "we try to trace that paper hat. It could give us another possible witness."

"Witness to what?"

"That's what we're trying to find out, isn't it?"

Chapter Twenty-One

Lowell watched the rain.

"It's slowing down. We'll go out again in a little while. We're going to look for another graveyard."

It didn't matter. She had given up hope that anyone would see them. They could go out among people all they wanted, and no one would pay attention or realize their plight.

He kept looking at her. She did not like the way he looked. He was ready for another power play, and she knew what it would be this time.

She could tell him she had a disease. She would have to think of one. He would probably kill her for thwarting him—unless he still needed her to drive the car.

Until he found a new identity. Then he wouldn't need her at all.

Please make it quick. All of us at once, so the children won't be afraid. Three bullets in a row, and don't miss. Don't botch it.

She imagined them lined up together. . . .

She stayed in the car, cradling Darren, trying to muffle his coughs. Candy lay next to him so she could share the blanket. She was subdued and apathetic.

Better that way. Maybe she wouldn't miss her life when it ended.

Lowell sauntered back from the barn door and stood looking in through the open tailgate at Darren.

"Still got that cough, huh?"

His voice was smooth. No hint of the fact that he had almost killed because of that cough.

"He's feverish," said Kate. "He feels hot. He's very sick, Lowell."

As if he would care. She hadn't meant to say it quite like that.

In fact, she should not have said it at all. Lowell's eyes narrowed.

She glared back at him. He must understand that if anything happened to her children, she would be of no use to him at all. She and the children were one.

"You," he said to her. "Come on upstairs."

Candy raised her head. "No, Mommy."

Now it was coming.

"It's all right, sweetheart."

She couldn't. Not with him. Never.

But she couldn't make him angry. She eased herself off the back deck, trying not to disturb Darren. Candy sat up with her, watching her leave.

I can't, thought Kate. *I'll be sick.*

Play along with him. Don't make him angry.

But if he gets what he wants—then he'll be through with me. I should leave him hungry.

Hungry or angry?

She looked back. She could see both their faces, Darren's through the glass, Candy's leaning out of the tailgate.

Did they know what was happening?

"Listen," she said, when they were out of the children's hearing, "I'd love to do what you want, but I think you should know, I'm not well."

He stared at her. "What are you talking about? Woman trouble?"

Suddenly she knew what to say.

"I'm pregnant."

"You're what?"

"I'm expecting a child. I'm three months pregnant. I could have a miscarriage and bleed all over the place."

Again the eyes narrowed. His mouth lifted into a grimace of disgust.

"You bitch," he said.

"I—I'm *sorry*."

It wasn't true. She could deny it.

"Lowell—"

"You fucking bitch."

As though in a dream, she watched his arm pull back. Watched the blow aimed at her face.

She was falling backward. She had forgotten they were on the stairs. Wildly she grabbed for the wall, the rail. Grabbed the air as she was flung into space.

Until her head struck the wooden floor below.

Chapter Twenty - Two

Again Hennessy and Rizzo combed the mall, this time inquiring as to the origin of the tissue-paper hats.

Finally someone remembered. "Oh, yes, I know what you mean. It was a guy named Griggs."

Jack Griggs, they learned, worked as a checker at the Food World supermarket. He was also an amateur magician and had been dressed in a clown suit, performing his tricks for the Circus Day festivities.

"I think," said Hennessy as they walked back down the mall toward Food World, "we're going to wear a groove in this floor before we're finished."

They found Jack Griggs getting ready to leave for his break. He was a tall, slender man with a thin face and a thatch of light brown hair. They identified themselves, and he gave them a puzzled smile.

"Yes, sirs, what can I do for you?"

"We'd like to ask you a few questions," Hennessy said, "about Saturday. I understand you were part of the entertainment."

Griggs looked around to see if anybody was listening. "That's right. Why, is something wrong?"

Hennessy eased him away from the cash register. "Sorry to interfere with your break. This will only take a couple of minutes. I wonder if you remember this woman here, and these two kids. I understand you made a paper hat for the little girl."

Griggs took the photographs and studied them.

"Pink," he said.

"How's that?"

"It was a pink hat. I chose pink to match her coat. You know, this place was like a beach on the Fourth of July, but I remember them. The kid didn't have her front teeth, and she thought I was pretty exciting. She wanted her own dad to be a magician. The mother was a nice-looking woman. She admired the hat I made."

"Were they alone?" Hennessy asked. "The three of them?"

"As far as I can remember."

"Nobody was with them?"

"Uh—no. Why?"

"Anybody seem to be following them, or watching them, or paying attention to them in any way?"

"Not that I noticed. What happened? Did anything happen?"

"Just asking. Are you sure about that?"

"I'm sure I didn't notice. I can't be sure—hey, what's going on?"

"We don't know yet. Will you think about it? If you come up with anything, let me know."

"Are they missing or something?"

Hennessy pounced. "What makes you say that?"

"You said you aren't sure. If it was anything else, they'd be around someplace, and you'd be sure."

"Yeah, well, you're right. Oh, what the hell, the media's gotten hold of it anyway. Yeah, they've been missing since Saturday."

"Heck, they were nice kids. The mother, too. I hope nothing happened."

"So do I. But we'll find them. Here's my number if you think of anything else."

"And here's mine, if you need me." Griggs took a business card from his shirt pocket. " 'Mr. G.' the Magician," it said. "Magic for All Occasions."

He shook his head sadly as he handed it over. "I sure wish I could conjure up those people for you."

"Thanks." Hennessy slipped the card into his own pocket, and he and Rizzo turned to leave.

"What do you think?" asked Rizzo, who had been silently observing.

"Looks like this lead bombed out," said Hennessy. "Not that I didn't expect it. You got any ideas about where to go from here?"

They put in a call to headquarters and found a message waiting for them. The tan station wagon had been traced. It was a Vermont registration.

Hennessy made a note of the license number.

"Vermont registration," he reported.

"Hell," said Rizzo, "the way I heard it, anybody can get a Vermont registration for the asking. At least they used to."

"It happens to *be* Vermont. They got an address, but the people just left for Europe. Which explains, I guess, why their car was at the airport."

"I wonder how come they didn't notice their plates were changed. Unless it was nighttime. Did you know you can't see colors at night?"

"I," said Hennessy, "am aware of that, except under bright lights you can. Maybe they didn't happen to look. What the hell's that guy doing here?"

"What guy?"

"Armstrong. He's circling the parking lot."

"Trying to find a space."

"He's not shopping, Rizzo."

Ted had driven the distance twice from the railroad to the Brookside Mall. It was exactly half a mile. Next to the

153

railroad, just before the Saltport station, was an abandoned warehouse. They could have hidden there, he
thought. They could have seen it from the train, and
jumped off and hidden there. It might have made more
sense than staying with the train and risking notice from
a conductor, so that by the time they got to the city, an
alarm would have gone out and the stations would be
watched.

Still, that warehouse was awfully close to the railroad,
only one stop beyond where the getaway car was found.
If he were the police, he would have searched it.

He tried to call Hennessy, who, as usual, was out.
Working on the case, he hoped. At least they were treat-
ing it right, like a missing-persons case. They didn't just
assume she had gone off somewhere with the kids.

He needed help, but he couldn't think where to turn.
He was terrified of the press. Still, he kind of liked that
young reporter. This had been his idea, too, a possible
connection with the bank robbery.

It was probably farfetched, but it seemed worth a try.
No trace had been found of the two gunmen, and it
wasn't far to the mall. What better place to lose yourself
than in a crowd of people who are all intent on something
else? They could have hidden there overnight, if they
could evade the watchmen and the cleaning people.

He put in a call to the Saltport *Herald* and asked for
Boyd Potter.

"Potter?" they echoed in surprise. Nobody asked for
Potter.

"I want Potter," Ted insisted. "This is personal and
confidential."

They gave him Potter.

"Can you talk?" asked Ted. "Nobody listening in?"

Potter snickered. "She's tied up right now."

"I've been thinking about what you said. About that
bank robbery. I can't get hold of the police right now, but

154

I want to follow that up as fast as possible. Do you have any more information?"

"Hey, look, I'll meet you," Potter offered.

"That's great. Will you be alone?"

"Yes, she's working on a story. I—uh, I'll have to tell you about that."

Potter left the office on foot, and Ted picked him up around the corner.

"Do you get to write stories, too?" Ted asked. "You can have an exclusive, if anything turns up."

Potter looked surprised. "I wasn't even thinking of that. I was mostly trying to figure out what could have happened to your family."

They stopped outside a luncheonette. Potter went in and ordered two coffees, which he brought out to the car. They thought they would be fairly invisible in the car.

"You couldn't get hold of Hennessy?" Potter asked. "Then you probably don't know they traced the phony car. The one with your license plates. It comes from Vermont."

"*Vermont?* Oh my God, they're going to Canada."

"They'll get extradited. I mean, the guys who knocked off the bank."

"Oh, hell. Remember that case where somebody shot a policeman, and then he kidnapped a woman to get her car and fled to Canada?"

"And she was found dead," Potter said helpfully. "Oh, shit, I'm sorry. But it doesn't mean—He tried to disguise himself as a woman, remember? Maybe these guys are trying to disguise themselves with a phony family."

"They won't need a phony family indefinitely," groaned Ted.

"My mother always said, don't borrow trouble."

"How did you find out about Vermont?"

"We have spies at police headquarters."

"State police, too? Everywhere?"

"Everywhere. That's what spies are for. Don't forget, my paper's interested in the bank robbery, too. So what do we do now?"

"We try to get hold of Hennessy," said Ted.

"Don't wait for Hennessy. Get the guys who are working on the robbery."

He let Potter make the call. They would talk to a reporter, but not to him. Not a relative of the victims. Everybody came ahead of the victims, he thought bitterly.

Potter returned with triumphant news.

"They got an ID on one of the crooks. It's an Al Torrey. He lives in Queens."

"How did they find that out?"

"Fingerprints, but not in the bank. I think he tinkered with the getaway car."

"Anything else? Do you know where they went?"

"Not yet. They're trying to find out who the other guy was. Torrey did a stretch upstate. He might have picked up some friends there."

"They've got my family. I can feel it."

"Do you get vibes, too? Hey, look, now that they know who he is, maybe they can figure out where he might have gone. People have patterns, you know. They go to areas they're familiar with, or they follow up some special interest, even when they're trying to hide."

"Yeah," said Ted. "His special interest would be money, and he's already followed that up. But I think I'm right. I think they came here. Just one stop on the railroad. How do I get the police to consider that?"

"If I was them, I would have gone two or three stops."

"Not if you looked out and saw that warehouse, and you knew if you went on into the city, they'd be waiting for you."

"I guess you're right. I guess they'd be jittery and looking for the best place to hide. You know what? I'm going to try a story."

Ted was interested. "Will they let you print it?"

"Sure. It's kind of a small paper. They're always looking for stuff. With anything like that holdup, or your family disappearing, they go crazy. They'd go even crazier over a tie-in."

"As long as it wakes up the police." Ted started his car and drove back toward the *Herald* offices.

"You don't want the police to waste all their time barking up the wrong tree," Potter warned him, "in case it *is* a wrong tree."

"Don't you think they'd be too intelligent for that? I just want them to consider it."

"They probably will." Potter got out of the car. "I'll keep in touch."

As soon as he entered the building, Potter remembered that he had forgotten to warn the man about Sandra's story. He raced back to the door, but Armstrong had already left.

"Uh-oh," he muttered and went to his desk.

Sandra spun her chair to face him. "Where did you run off to?"

She wasn't working on anything at the moment. She must have finished the story and handed it in.

"I went to interview a cat up a tree," he said.

"Funny. Funny." She opened her compact, powdered her nose and patted her hair.

She wasn't usually so vain. He wondered what had happened.

"I'm off," she told him. "I don't need you this time."

"Where are you off to?"

"Wouldn't you like to know." When he didn't answer, she tossed over her shoulder, "To see the police. They've

157

got some nutty idea those two bank robbers might have abducted the Armstrong family."

His story. He felt as though she had kicked him in the gut.

But finding the Armstrongs was more important than who got to write the story, and coverage, any coverage, would bring out all the guns.

Still, he couldn't help a snide bit of revenge. "Which one were you fixing your hair for?" he asked.

She waggled her hips. "I thought the young one was kind of cute."

"He's married," said Potter, remembering a ring on Rizzo's finger.

She stamped out of the room, and he grinned to himself. It was almost worth the loss of his story.

Chapter Twenty·Three

Kate woke to find Candy bending over her. Candy was stroking her face and weeping. Darren stood wide-eyed, his blanket trailing on the floor.

"What happened?" asked Kate. Her voice came out a whisper.

She tried to move. Pains shot through her neck and shoulders. Her head was broken, she knew it.

"He hit you," Candy sobbed.

"Who did?"

"Lowell."

Kate looked around and saw the barn. She had forgotten that she was there.

"Help me sit up."

Candy tugged ineffectually at her arm.

"*Wait.*"

Her arm was broken. No, maybe it wasn't. She rolled to her side and cautiously tested it.

At least she could move, but the pain was everywhere. She felt sick to her stomach.

"Did he do anything after he hit me?" she asked.

"He kicked you. With his foot." Candy began to cry again.

"Anything else?"

"Then he went upstairs."

It must have just happened. She could hear him up there, his feet on the hollow floor.

"Mommy, I wish we could go away right now."

"I'm not sure I can even walk." Kate managed to stand up, clutching Candy for support. "Darren, get back in the car and keep warm."

Still resting her weight on Candy's shoulder, she staggered toward the car to sit down. If only she could have gotten the key. If she had gone along with him, it might have been possible. He might have fallen asleep.

Defending my honor, she thought bitterly. But it hadn't been that. It had been revulsion, not only at the physical intimacy, but the thought of giving in to his greed for power. She had to have something left of herself.

She should have given in bodily but divorced her mind. That was what they did. That was how prisoners and hostages survived. Keep the inner core of yourself intact. She must remember.

She contemplated the back deck but knew she could never lift herself up onto it, never lie on that hard floor. Instead she crawled into the front seat under the wheel. Her own place. It was her car. He could hijack it, even wreck it or set fire to it, but it was still her car. Still herself. The children were hers, too. He hadn't created them, even though he thought he owned them all.

He was coming down the stairs. He paused when he saw her in the car. An ugly look twisted his face.

She mustn't defy him. Let him think he had the power he wanted. Let him know that he had hurt her.

She lay against the steering wheel, careful not to blow the horn. She was not pretending. He *had* hurt her. He did have physical power.

"The rain stopped," he said. "We're going to try another graveyard, down in that town."

He couldn't be serious. Did he expect her to drive?

"Lowell, I'm all broken inside."

"You're going to do like I say." He reached for his pocket.

Then he glanced at the children. That was his real weapon. He would hurt the children.

I can't drive, she thought. Her arms were useless, weak, and shaking. She still felt sick. She might throw up.

"I said let's go!"

He looked again at the children. At Candy. A light came into his eyes.

No! No, not Candy! Oh, my God.

"You'll have to give me the keys," she said.

There were tears in her voice. She forced them down. He mustn't know he had reached her.

But he did know.

He tossed her the keys, then got in beside her. He was almost smiling. He had won, and he knew it.

"If you want me to drive for you," she said meekly, "then you shouldn't beat me up like that. You could have broken my arm, or my neck, and we'd be stuck here."

"Shut up, bitch."

He had called her "bitch." It was coming back to her now. She had told him she was pregnant. Some men, she remembered, especially the more ignorant ones, felt revulsion at the thought of touching a pregnant woman. That was what had done it. She had revolted and thwarted him at the same time. And had paid for it.

When she drove out of the barn, she saw that he was right. The rain had stopped, but drops still fell from the trees. Bumping along the overgrown path, she had to turn on the windshield wipers.

Her stomach churned. She could stop, open the door and throw up. He would hit her again. He would probably kill her for stopping where their car might be seen

161

from the road. A car in that obviously deserted place might arouse curiosity. On the highway, no one would think about it.

She was glad when they reached the highway. It was smoother, but now she had to drive faster, and she couldn't concentrate. She was dizzy. Her head swam and she could scarcely see.

Please, God, just let me make it.

"Where are we going?" she asked.

"I told you! That place where we made the phone call."

She could not remember his telling her. She had headed in the right direction without thinking.

"Could we stop at the store?" she asked. "I need—"

"What?"

"Something for this pain."

"Shit." He spat out of the window.

She had forgotten to clock the mileage. The road seemed to go on for years. She faded and pulled herself back. She let everything else go, except her concentration on the road.

I'm going to die, she thought. *I'm really going to die.*

But she wouldn't, because of the children. She couldn't leave them with him.

Something in her unconscious mind found the road that turned down the mountainside. Something reminded her to put the car into low gear, since her leg was too weak to hold the brake. Something was keeping her alive.

When they reached the village he made her stop for gas, but again refused a trip to the store.

"We've got to find that graveyard before it gets dark," he said.

It made sense, in his terms, but she couldn't stand the pain. Her entire body was filled with stabbing pain. He probably didn't want to admit that it was he who had inflicted it.

"I thought you said the early morning was best," she reminded him. "People might be visiting the graves now. They'll wonder what we're doing."

"So, we're visiting a grave. Go up that road there."

The road led out of the village. When they had driven for two miles, he ordered her to turn back. They tried another road, and then another. She had not thought the village was big enough to have so many means of access. On the third, they found a cemetery.

"You see?" he exclaimed. "I was right."

The drive into the cemetery was blocked by a chain. They had to park on the road and walk in. He didn't like that, didn't like leaving the car out where it could be seen.

The air was raw, cold, and windy, and no one else was visiting the graves. The cold wind revived her, somehow deadening the pain, or distracting her.

Candy shivered in her thin pink windbreaker. Kate offered her own jacket. Candy shook her head.

"Couldn't they stay in the car?" asked Kate. "They don't read much anyway, and Darren's going to get worse—"

"Forget it."

He didn't trust them. She hadn't even thought that they might talk to anyone.

They all fanned out to examine the stones. She kept Darren with her, trying to shield him from the wind. It was only a matter of minutes before she felt the wetness of the grass inside her shoes. Darren's were soaked. He could take them off during the night, but they probably wouldn't dry in the cold, damp air.

She walked through row after row, glancing at the stones, with Darren coughing beside her. She glanced at a date and walked on. Then turned back.

"Lowell!"

"Yeah?"

163

"You could pass for twenty-nine, couldn't you?"

He bounded toward her. The name on the stone was Peter Faulkner. His birthdate was four years earlier than Lowell's, and he had died at the age of two.

"Do you think that's okay?" she asked.

He stood looking at it and didn't answer.

"It's only four years," she said. "Four years is nothing."

He dug in his pocket and pulled out a memo pad and a felt-tipped pen that he had taken from the glove compartment. He wrote down the name and the dates. He wrote everything that was on the stone, including "Beloved son of Danton and Grace."

"It's sad," she said. "Their little baby."

"Shut up." He stuffed the pad into his pocket and folded his arms.

Then he said, "I have to check out the family."

"How are you going to do that?"

"Phone book."

"But what do you have to check?"

He stared at her in disgust. "Where's your brains? I have to find out if they're still around here, don't I? This isn't such a big place. Do you think I want to get caught?"

She was glad they had found something. Glad they could leave the graveyard and get Darren out of the cutting wind.

She drove back to the village. The grocery store had closed. All the stores had closed. It was past eight o'clock, and Main Street lay in a twilight gloom under heavy clouds.

"Go down to the end there." He pointed toward the mountain.

"I thought you wanted to look up something."

"I said go down to the end there."

When she reached the last group of buildings, he

stopped her. She saw that they were in front of a hardware and appliance shop.

"Go in there." He pointed to an alley that ran to the
back of the store.

By the rear delivery entrance was a small paved area.
She parked under a willow tree, and Lowell got out of the
car. He rapped on one of the back-seat windows, ordering
Darren to go with him.

"But he's—" Kate began.

He pointed a finger at her. "You better not move."

Darren looked back at her pleadingly, then up at
Lowell as they approached the store. She watched
Lowell peer through a window and knock on the glass.
When nothing happened, he climbed a step to the back
door, squatted in front of it, and seemed to be doing
something with the lock.

"Is he going to hurt Darren?" Candy asked.

"He'd better not," said Kate. "If he hurts either of you,
I'll kill him. I'll figure out a way."

She saw the door open and Lowell and Darren disap-
pear.

She did not know when they would be back. She could
do nothing but wait. There was not a telephone in sight,
or even a person, although she heard voices somewhere in
the distance.

Besides, he could probably see her through that window.

She felt her wrists and tried to see her hands in the
growing darkness. Her left hand felt as though he might
have stepped on it. Was it only that afternoon that she
had been hurt? And then there was yesterday . . .

She tried to remember what day it was.

She wondered if Ted was looking for her. By now he
must have talked to her mother, learned she wasn't there,
and called the police. And what would they do? Would

they really try to find her? Where would they start?

If she were the police, she wouldn't have any idea of where or how to begin. It was a great big planet, and she could be anywhere. How would they narrow it down?

In the gloom, she saw the store's rear door open. The building was white, and the door made a dark rectangle. Lowell and Darren came toward her with their arms full of packages.

"We broke in the store," Darren said when they reached the car.

Lowell opened the tailgate, helped Darren up and slid a long, thin carton in beside him. Kate could not see what it said on the carton. She thought it might be a rifle. He covered it with the beach blanket.

Then he got into the front seat, carrying a bulkier box. On the outside was a picture of a powerful, two-speaker radio.

"Go to the phone booth now," he said.

"The phone booth?"

"The one by the gas station!"

There had been a directory, he said, hanging from a chain in the booth.

The gas station, too, was closed, its office lit by a thin fluorescent light. The phone booth had a light inside. The rest of the area was in shadows. As soon as Lowell got out of the car, she turned around to be sure Darren was all right.

He was chattering excitedly, telling his sister about the break-in.

"He made the door get open, and he didn't have a key!"

"Maybe it was already open," Candy said.

"No, it wasn't. Then we got a gun and a radio and some bullets."

"Did he talk to you?" asked Kate.

"Yes. He's nice."

"He is not!" Candy cried. "He hurt Mommy, and he hurt me, too."

"And me."

Someone rapped on the front window. She turned quickly, thinking it was Lowell. Candy made a gurgling sound.

She saw a uniform. A badge.

She stared. She felt as though she had been kicked again. Her heart began to pound.

She rolled down the window. The officer asked, "You people waiting for something? The last bus already left."

She turned helplessly to Lowell. He was watching her from the booth. He held the receiver to his ear, and he looked rigid.

"What bus?" she asked.

"Well, okay, I thought you might be waiting for the bus. I wanted to tell you it already came and went."

"No, we—got lost. My friend is trying to call somebody."

"Where do you want to go?"

She had a dazed impression of blue eyes and a mustache. She couldn't tell whether he was suspicious or trying to be helpful.

"Uh—" Oyster Drive. It was the only address she could think of. But there were no oysters in this part of Vermont.

"It's a—a place called Ivy Lane."

The street next to Oyster Drive.

"I'm afraid I don't know that," he said. "I should know it. Who are the people you're going to see?"

"Well . . . it's not exactly in this town. We got lost, so he's calling the people to come and meet us."

She glanced again at Lowell. He was still pretending to talk. The booth door was only half glass, but she knew he had his gun ready.

"We'll be all right, honestly," she said.

"Okay, then. If you need any help, I'll be around." The trooper returned to his car.

Candy leaned forward. "Mommy, why didn't you *tell* him?"

Kate wilted against the door. "I was scared. I didn't see him coming."

"But why didn't you tell him?"

"Because he would have killed us."

He.

She looked at Lowell. She pleaded with him.

As soon as the policeman drove away, Lowell stormed out of the booth and into the car. She felt his breath on her face.

"You little rat, what did you tell him?"

The gun. The gun in her ribs.

"I—*nothing.* I didn't. Candy, I didn't!"

Candy screamed. Kate saw that he was pointing the gun at Darren.

"I didn't!" She grabbed for the gun. "I said we were lost. I said you were making a phone call. I *did.*"

"It's true!" shrieked Candy.

He lowered his gun. His fist cracked against her face. She felt the blow, but no pain. There was only blackness and light.

She shook her head. Then the pain came.

"I really didn't ... tell ... him. Can't you see? He drove away."

Lowell watched her, silently.

Then he asked, "That the truth?"

"Yes." She held her hand to her face.

He turned to Candy. There was no audible exchange, but Candy must somehow have confirmed it.

"That better be the truth."

She nodded. "Please don't hurt me again."

168

"Let's get out of here."

She started the car. Her leg trembled. She couldn't control it. Couldn't hold it on the gas.

When they began to climb the mountain, she forced down her foot and hurried toward the safety of the barn.

Chapter Twenty · Four

Hennessy was working overtime, alone. There wasn't much reason for being at home. The kids were all married and leading their own lives. Ruthie had gone to Scranton to help her ninety-year-old mother move to a nursing home. He wished he could have been there with her, but that was out of the question, especially with this case going on.

He sat in his car and tried to think beyond the only two leads, both of which had bombed.

Tomorrow the story would break in the Saltport *Herald*. Maybe some witnesses would come forward. Maybe not. Maybe there weren't any. A white station wagon and three people had simply disappeared. In the Bermuda Triangle, you could understand it. They'd have sunk to the bottom of the sea.

Maybe they went off a bridge, he thought. *Maybe they're down there someplace.*

But there were no bridges between their home and the mall, and they had definitely been traced to the mall.

He didn't know what had happened, but it wasn't any accident. There were those license plates showing up in Boston. They could have been stolen—but why? The car on which the plates had been found belonged to a middle-aged Vermont couple who checked out as law-abiding people. More likely, it was their plates that had been stolen for use on the Armstrong car.

The two cars must have crossed paths at some point. He had the Vermont police asking the couple's daughter what route her parents had taken to Boston. It must have been somewhere along there, but that didn't mean the Armstrong car was still in the area. He had put out a bulletin for a white station wagon with the Vermont plate number. In the meantime . . .

There were his two leads. He could try them again. Try a different set of questions. Sometimes people saw something and didn't know they saw it.

He had the druggist's home address and phone number. What he really needed was a cellular phone. Lacking that, he drove to the bowling alley, where he knew there would be a pay phone.

As soon as he started moving, he noticed a car on his tail. He watched it with interest. When he made a sudden turn down a side street, the car followed.

He entered the bowling alley parking lot under a bright bank of lights. The car still followed, but he recognized it now. It was those reporters from the *Herald.* Working overtime, like himself. He got out of his car and went into the building. From the corner of his eye, he saw the young man follow him.

He slipped into a booth and called the druggist's number. He counted twelve rings. Long enough for somebody to get in from the patio or out of the shower. Maybe it was the druggist's bowling night and he was right there, a few feet away. Hennessy took out Mr. G's card and tried that number.

The phone was answered by Mrs. G. She asked who was calling.

"I'm a police officer," Hennessy said and identified himself. He heard a gasp. Probably she thought there had been an accident.

Finally he had Jack Griggs on the phone. He asked a question he should have thought of the first time.

"Look, Griggs, was anybody with you that day at the mall? Anybody who might have seen the Armstrong family and noticed anything?"

"My daughter was with me," Griggs replied. "I could ask her."

"Hold it. Let me do the asking, okay? Don't say anything till I get there, about five or ten minutes."

When he left the booth, the young reporter quickly terminated what was probably a dummy call and followed him.

The Griggses lived in a small house on the edge of Saltport, not far from the mall. Jack Griggs opened the door. His wife hovered in the background, a tall, handsome woman with a worried expression. Evidently she had not been told what this was all about. Hennessy was just as glad. It meant the daughter's answers would be more spontaneous, although probably they would lead nowhere. Everybody, it seemed, had seen the Armstrongs, but nobody knew what happened to them. It figured. Why should anybody know?

Griggs called his daughter. For some reason, Hennessy had expected at least a teenager, but Christine was only ten. She had short blond hair, big blue eyes, and wore a pink bathrobe over her pajamas.

In the living room, a small boy sat on the floor watching television. The Griggses turned over their kitchen for the interview. Both parents stayed near the doorway, which was all right with Hennessy, as long as they kept quiet and didn't try to prompt. He showed Christine the pictures of all three Armstrongs and asked if she had seen them.

"Oh—yes, I remember that girl. My dad made a hat for her, and she thought I was lucky."

"Lucky?"

172

Christine blushed. "Well, she didn't exactly say that, but she wished she could do what I was doing, helping my dad. She said, 'I never have any fun.' Kids say that a lot."

"Yeah. Right. Anything else?"

"She said she wished her dad was a magician." Christine smiled happily at the memory.

"Did you see anybody with them? Any other person with these people?"

"Yes, there was him." She pointed to the Armstrong son in the picture. "And their mother. I guess it was their mother. That lady." She pointed to the wife.

Pretty good memory, he thought. She even remembered what the girl had said.

"Was anybody else there? Did you see anybody following them, or watching them?"

"Not then," Christine replied, "but after."

Hennessy felt the hair rise at the back of his neck. "After what?"

"After, when they went out."

"Out where?"

"Out of the mall. That was a little while after. We were down by the door, the one where Baskin-Robbins is, and I saw them go out."

"What happened?"

"Well, it was raining. The lady tried to open her umbrella. And there was a man. He was standing near the door. He was there when they went out. I saw the lady look at him, and then they all went together."

"Where did they go?" Hennessy asked, trying to keep his voice steady.

"I don't know. I couldn't see, but they were out in the parking lot. He was a little bit in back of them. Then my dad went somewhere else and I had to go with him."

"Can you tell me what the man looked like?"

"Umm . . . just his back. He had a black coat. A jacket.

And a black hat." She pulled her hands tightly over her hair. "A knit one, not a real hat, I mean."

"What did his face look like?"

"I couldn't see his face."

"Anything else? What kind of pants did he have on?"

"I can't remember."

"That's okay, young lady. You don't know what a help you've been. I thank you."

As he left the house, he said to Christine's parents, "Don't be too surprised if some people come bothering you from the newspaper. They're following me all over, but you don't have to talk to them if you don't want to."

"Would there be any problem for Chris if we did?" asked Griggs.

"I hardly think so. She didn't see the guy's face, and if I'm correct, our birds have migrated by now."

"Here he comes," said Sandra as Hennessy trotted down the steps. "Wait and see if he radios. Otherwise we'll go in."

Hennessy got into his car but didn't start it. They picked up the call on their own receiver.

Listening to it, Potter felt a glow of satisfaction. For once in his life, he had been right about something. Even the black jacket checked out. But of course there could be a million guys with black jackets.

"They couldn't still be alive," he said.

"Shut up, will you? I'm listening."

The call was finished. He asked, "Now what happens?"

"Now we pay a visit to Armstrong."

"What for?"

"Reactions, Pothead! That's what it's all about. That's news."

"But what if he doesn't know yet? The police only just found out, and they never tell—"

"*We* are going to do the telling."

"Sandra, is that ethical?"

"Screw ethical. This is a story!"

"I mean, what if the police don't want you—"

"Running off at the mouth? Well, screw the police. Don't quote me on that."

They found Armstrong at home, trying valiantly to watch television. Bullets and bombs were flying somewhere in another room, but Armstrong couldn't have cared less about make-believe troubles.

"I really have nothing to say to you," he told them.

"*We* have something for *you*," Sandra announced, pushing her way in. "You know, we can pick up police calls on our radio."

Armstrong didn't move, but Potter thought he saw a transformation. He thought it was solid goosebumps.

"There's this little kid who was at the mall," Sandra went on. "She saw a man waiting when your family went out that day. A man in a black jacket. He went with them to their car."

Armstrong looked baffled. He couldn't seem to put it all together.

"One of the bank robbers had a black jacket!" she crowed. "We were right!"

"We were? Oh, hell. *Why?*"

"Get with it, Armstrong. He was probably hanging around there waiting for a car. Waiting for somebody who couldn't run or fight back. Like a mother with little kids. How about that?"

For some reason, Armstrong didn't seem to know what was expected of him. He put his hand to his forehead and took a step backward. He appeared to be reeling.

Then he said, "Get out of here, will you?"

"Oh, come *on.* You must have something to say."

"Not to you."

"Don't forget, big boy, the public has a right to know."

"Sandra," said Potter, "that's not what it means."

"Shut up, Potts. Listen, Armstrong, we have more. We know where they probably went."

"You what?"

"Just what I said. It's possible they might not still be there, but at least we know the direction. The car that was found with your plates on it presumably traveled east through southern Vermont, maybe Route Nine, to get to Boston. The people spent the night at a motel in Brattleboro, so that could place your car in the area sometime Sunday night or Monday morning." She grinned and stood with her pencil poised, waiting for the all-important comment.

Armstrong took another step backward. He turned and stumbled into the living room, to a floor-to-ceiling built-in bookcase. He ran his hand along the bottom shelf, which was the tallest, and pulled out something wide and floppy. Potter recognized it as the Rand McNally Road Atlas.

Sandra watched in fascination as he flipped through the pages.

"It's under New Hampshire," Potter volunteered. "They're both together, in the N's."

Sandra glared at him, but he was right. Armstrong found the page and began tracing along it with his finger.

Sandra moistened her lips. "What are you doing?"

He traced it again. Then he turned to another page and traced that. Sandra's eyes bulged.

He closed the atlas and looked at them fiercely.

"Out," he said. "Get out of my house."

Sandra took Potter's sleeve and led him to the door. They were not just leaving quietly, he knew that. Sandra didn't give up.

Outside, she hustled him into the car.

"As soon as we're out of the driveway," she said, "pull back and turn off your lights."

"Pull back where?"

"Just *back*, dummy. See that house there? Park in front of it and wait."

It was two houses down from the Armstrongs'. When he reached it, he pulled over to the curb and switched off his engine.

"What are you going to be doing?" he asked.

"Me? I'm waiting right here with you. I wouldn't miss this for anything. It's the story of a lifetime."

Potter said, "He wouldn't really go to Vermont."

"You think not?" She opened the glove compartment and pawed through it until she found a map of New England. With the help of a penlight that was handily in her purse, she proceeded to study it.

"Sandra, we're not—we're not—are we?"

At the Armstrong house, a light went on in an upstairs room.

"But they might not be there now," he said. "Probably they're not." He was sure they were dead.

"Potts, our job is to go where the action is, whatever that action is. Right now, he's the action."

A shadow moved back and forth across the light. Then the light went off. Sandra bounced excitedly.

"This is insane," he told her. "You do know that."

One by one the other lights went off. Probably the television, too. Through his open window, Potter thought he heard the sound of a garage door.

He saw lights blaze on a tree at the side of the house.

"Look," he tried, "we can't just go off like this. I don't have my pajamas."

"We're not going there to sleep, Pothead."

"My razor."

"I'll buy you one."

He heard the garage door close. Then two headlights appeared in the driveway, traveling rapidly.

"Hold it," she said. "Wait till he makes his turn."

Armstrong whipped around the corner and out toward

Arnold Carver Road. Potter started after the taillights.

"What if I lose him?"

"Just keep going. I'll tell you the way. Aim for Brattleboro. That's probably where he's headed."

Vermont. He had some vague idea that if they crossed the Throgs Neck Bridge, there might be a road leading north.

"How far is it?" he asked.

"I don't know. A few hundred miles. I figure it shouldn't take more than six or seven hours."

"I hope you know I can't drive very well when I'm asleep."

"I told you, Potts, no sleeping. I might feed you now and then, if Armstrong stops, but *no sleeping*."

Chapter Twenty - Five

The children were asleep in the back of the car. She sat in front, watching Lowell fiddle with his radio. He was angry at first, as though he blamed her for the appearance of the trooper. She had tried to be strong. Tried not to cry.

Later, when she helped him put the batteries into his radio, he had mellowed. But he still worried.

"Think he saw the license plates?"

"I really don't know," she answered. "He didn't say anything. He just wondered what we were doing there, since the station was closed and the last bus went."

"We were making a phone call. What's wrong with that?"

"Nothing. I guess he accepted it."

But why had she told him all that nonsense about getting lost? Again she had talked too much.

"Can't stay here now," he said.

"Where will you go?"

She didn't care where he went. She wanted the other question answered, the one she hadn't asked.

"Could go to Mexico," he said.

"It's a long way. How will you get there from here without anybody seeing you?"

"Hell with it." He pushed away the radio. "I've got to

get out of here. Now. Get that stuff from upstairs and let's go."

"Please. I couldn't drive now. I can't drive all night, the way I feel now."

"Huh!" he snorted, as she began to shake. He noticed the shaking.

Grudgingly, he said, "Okay, then, tomorrow morning, before it gets light. That's when we move."

"North or south?"

"And we're dumping the kids."

"No!" Oh, not the children. She knew what he meant to do.

"What good are kids?" he asked.

"They're—mine. They're my children. You can't—"

He was breathing hard. Another power trip. She would have to think of something.

"I know what it means to you." She would try understanding. "They remind you of your brother. That's why you don't want them."

"Bullshit. They're trouble, that's why." His voice was harsh.

"Yes, I realize that. I know they're trouble for you. But, please. Let me have just that. My children."

"Damn the kids. I'll go by myself."

"I'll drive you, Lowell. I'll take you anywhere you want, if you'll let me bring the children. I promise to keep them from making trouble."

He sneered. "Yeah? How?"

How? They were children. Unpredictable.

"We can both keep them in line."

She didn't want him to discipline her children or even go near them. But he needed it. The power.

"Sometimes," she went on, "it's very hard to—to feel that you're making an impact. That you matter to people. Or at least to someone."

"What are you talking about, bitch?"

"I'm talking about both of us. We both need to feel that we matter. You've been stepped on, and so have I. My husband—"

He picked up the radio again and twirled the knob. She heard voices and music, alternating. He kept the sound low, and she talked over it.

"My husband does the same kind of thing that people have done to you," she said. "I run his household, raise his children, take care of everybody when they're sick, and he acts as if it's all a lot of busy work to keep me amused, not anything important, like what he does."

"What's he do?" Lowell continued to play the radio.

"He works for an aircraft company."

"What, a big shot?"

"Well, it's mostly the data part. You know, computers. He—"

"What's that got to do with me?"

She could not remember what it had to do with him. Her head ached, and she had lost track of the point she was trying to make.

She had only wanted to show that she understood him. To make him identify with her, or the other way around. That they were together.

"I think it's a human need," she said, "to feel that you count for something. You haven't had much chance to feel that way, and neither have I, the way he treats me. He has no respect for what I do. He trivializes it. Maybe kids seem trivial while they're kids, but they grow up to be people. They're the next generation of aircraft manufacturers."

She had wandered again. Talking about herself. Maybe it would help him understand her better.

"So we'll go to Mexico," she said. "We'll be like your family."

"Shit. Who needs it?"

"Nobody will ever know it's you. You'll look like a man traveling with a wife and kids."

"If your old man came back, they'll be looking for you, too. I should have done it sooner."

She felt as though he had struck her again. He was determined.

She tried one more time.

"But you can't—do it here. If they happen to come here, they might find your friend. And if there are—any more—they'll know we were all together. Then it will be easier to trace you."

She knew what she wanted to say, but it wasn't coming out right.

"Do you know what I mean?" she begged. "If it's in a separate place—"

"Huh!"

He said no more than that. She thought he must have understood but couldn't tell whether he would go along with it. In any case, all it could do was buy a little more time. Maybe she could persuade him to keep the children alive until Mexico. Then, when they crossed the border . . . you had to have all sorts of papers to cross the border. . . .

She needed to be with them. She needed it more than sleep itself.

"I've got to get some rest, if we're going out early in the morning. It's—it's going to be a lot of driving. I need to feel well for it."

He turned back to the radio and didn't answer. She went around to the back of the car and opened the tailgate. Lifting herself up was hard, but finally she was inside. Gently moving Darren, she crawled between the children and lay down. She could feel both their bodies, and maybe if she were there, at least he wouldn't shoot them in their sleep. Or whatever he meant to do.

182

She found she was shaking again and tried to still it so it wouldn't wake them.

If only she could do something. But she was afraid to try. Afraid it wouldn't succeed. And then it would only be worse.

Especially for the children.

Chapter Twenty · Six

He had reached Brattleboro. It was pitch dark, sometime in the small hours of the morning. Brattleboro was dead.

For a while a car had been following him. He had thought it might be the reporters, but the car was gone now. He almost wished they were there. They might have had some ideas about what to do next. It had been a half-cocked, half-ass impulse, racing up here like this, but he had felt drawn, as if the imprint, the echo, of his family might still be somewhere along this route. He had to do what he could.

Besides, he didn't want to be around when Hennessy came to tell him they had found the bodies.

In an hour or so, it ought to be daylight. Until then, there was no sense in trying to find where anything was. He drove into an empty parking lot to try to catch some sleep.

It was a restaurant, closed for the night. Everything was closed. He rested against the window, feeling the chill of the glass, and closed his eyes.

Saturday, he thought. Saturday the horror had begun for them. Had it ended soon afterward? How long?

He was glad he had spent that night in his own room at the hotel.

But he had been with Elaine earlier. They had made love again. While Kate and the children . . .

He didn't want to think about it. He wouldn't, and probably he would never know for sure.

Never know. At least not *when*, even if they managed to find out what happened. If he hadn't gone on the trip . . .

There were always things like that. If only. You could torture yourself to death with it, but you couldn't change it. And you could never, never anticipate such things. It was part of life, he supposed.

No good. He couldn't sleep. He moved to the back seat and tried lying down. It was a little better but still not great, and anyway, he was too keyed up.

He opened his eyes when a light hit the car. It was probably a cop, checking for loiterers in the parking lot. He would tell them why he was there, and if they believed him, maybe they would help. Maybe not.

After a moment the light went away, and he was left alone with his thoughts.

Chapter Twenty·Seven

During the night, Kate's dreams kept waking her. Dreams that they were on the road, driving to Mexico. Dream after dream of the moving car, of seeing a tree or an embankment before them and being unable to stop.

She was finally, deeply asleep when Lowell woke her.

"Hey," he said from the front seat, "time to get moving."

She opened her eyes to solid darkness.

"Wake up."

"I'm awake."

The children stirred against her. She tried to move and found she was one massive ache. Against her face, the carpet was rough and gritty with beach sand.

"Let's go!"

Candy sat up. Kate raised herself until she rested on her hand.

I can do it. I have to do it.

She pushed open the unlatched tailgate and climbed out. Away from the warmth of her children, the air was cold. She shivered and steadied herself as her legs threatened to give way.

I can do it.

"Hey!" said Lowell. "Let's get started. Now!"

"I have to go outside for a minute."

"Why didn't you do that already? Hurry up!"

She waded through wet grass, around to the side of the barn. The night was chilly, but not bitter, and very fresh. In the distance, on the horizon, was a streak of light. The beginning of dawn.

She found some wet leaves and rubbed them on her face. She smoothed her hair and went back inside.

The children took their turn, while Lowell packed in the supplies and ran the flashlight over the floor to check for anything that might have fallen. Anything that could betray their presence there. He ordered Kate into the car and stood looking at the children.

They looked back at him. Darren, remembering Lowell's apparent friendliness when they broke into the store together, asked, "Are we going to McDonald's again?"

"Darren!" said Kate sharply.

He turned from one to the other in bewilderment. "But I'm hungry."

"You see?" said Lowell. "I told you they're trouble."

"Darren, *please*, just be quiet, *please*. It's very important."

It would do no good to remind Lowell that the boy was only four. That was the very thing he objected to.

Or to remind him that he had done the kidnapping. That it hadn't been their idea. In his own way, Lowell was as childish, as limited in his point of view, as Darren.

All she could do was say quietly, "Remember what I told you. If you want a ride to Mexico, we go as a family of four."

A silent, unreadable expression played across his face. Then he took a step toward the children. They cringed.

"Get in there," he said, waving his gun. They turned and scurried to their places in the car.

Kate drove out of the barn. Away from the cold, the

misery, and Torrey's ghost. Malevolent spirit.

Lowell made her keep her lights off. She inched forward, groping her way along the dirt lane.

"Move it, will you?"

"I really can't see where I'm going."

The lane seemed to stretch for miles, although it was really only yards. Finally they reached the end. The highway was pale gray and fuzzy with mist. She put on her headlights.

"Do you know where this road goes?" she asked. "I mean, eventually?"

"Shit. Just stay on it. Don't go near that town with the copper."

"I'll go wherever you say."

She meant it. She would be obliging and not argue with him. She would not ask for anything, except that he let her children live.

After a while, he muttered, "Damn sun's coming up."

She increased her speed. He had wanted to be farther away when daylight came.

Soon they would pass the way down to the village and leave it far behind. Then he would feel more relaxed, and so would the rest of them.

The day grew brighter. She turned off her lights.

Suddenly he whirled in his seat, grabbing her arm.

"*Stop*, will you?"

The car swerved, lurching from side to side. She slammed on the brake. "What hap—"

"Back there!"

She looked back. A small road ran off to their left, down the side of the mountain. She had thought it was a driveway.

"I didn't see—"

His grip hurt her arm. He shook it, as though to wake her.

"A cop car, damn you!"

188

"I—"

"Get back there. Get back to the barn. *Move it.*"

She had run into a ditch when he stopped her so abruptly. She put the car into reverse and tried to back out.

"They probably weren't looking for you," she said. "It must have been something—"

"Will you get out of here?"

"I'm trying to." She pulled forward to give herself a better angle. The ditch was muddy from yesterday's rain. She looked back and saw Candy watching, her little face taut with fear.

She shifted again and stepped on the gas as hard as she could. The car inched halfway out of the ditch, and then the wheels spun.

Lowell shouted to her. His hand was on the door. He was going to bolt through the woods.

"You'll never make it on foot," she told him.

Her mind cleared, and she realized that she was trying too hard, at too steep an angle. She put the car into low gear and drove forward, her right side in the ditch, faster and faster, until she could ease up onto the shoulder.

Clumsily, she turned the car. It was too long for an easy U-turn. Twice she had to stop and back, but there was no traffic on the road. With a spattering of pebbles, she was finally on her way to the barn, driving as fast as the law allowed.

I did it, she thought. *I did it.*

Lowell said nothing.

She asked, "Why do you want to go back there? Wouldn't it be better just to keep moving?"

"Hell, no, they'll see me on the road."

The license plates. Whoever owned those Vermont plates would surely have reported the switch by now. In the mirror, she noticed a small truck far behind them. She increased her speed.

She looked again. She had seen something else, on the edge of her vision. Candy, sliding across the back seat, pushing Darren against the door.

Her eyes met Candy's in the mirror. Candy gave a slight shake of her head. Kate was puzzled, but couldn't think about it now.

She outdistanced the truck. She prayed that there would be no more cars, that nothing would come from the other direction when they reached the barn road. It was still early and the traffic was light. The sun rose briefly and then disappeared behind clouds.

She was almost at the barn. She glanced into the mirror and then ahead. She had seen Candy's face looking wide-eyed and frozen. Probably carsick. She turned and plunged into the overgrown road, trying to get around the first bend before another car came along.

"We're making a path through here," she said. "I hope those weeds pop back fast."

"Just get in the barn," he answered heavily. "If the copper last night didn't see the plates, we're okay."

She drove into the barn, which they had left forever only a short time ago. It felt cold. Colder than the air outside. Probably it was Torrey, and it would always be there.

After she had parked and turned off the engine, she asked, "What are we going to do? We have hardly any food left."

"Shut up, will you?"

She wondered if he blamed her. He had wanted to leave last night. They could have been well away by now.

He was busy with his radio. Candy climbed over into the back deck and lay down.

Kate wanted to lie down, too. To sleep. To wake up back in Belle Harbor.

She turned to look at Lowell. They would have to get

him away. Somehow get him safe, and then maybe he would let them go.

"Mommy?" said Darren plaintively.

"Please!" she hissed, afraid that he would ask again for food.

"I don't feel good."

"I know, honey. I know you're sick. Why don't you lie down and try to sleep? And please don't talk. You'll hurt your throat."

He lay down on the back seat. If only they would sleep all day, stay quiet and show Lowell that they were no trouble.

"—in the area," barked the radio as Lowell turned it up. "Police believe they may have abducted a Long Island mother and her two children, who were reported missing by the woman's husband. However, according to a Long Island news report, the husband had been seeing another woman, and police are seeking to question him about the disappearance. In other news—"

"What 'in the area'?" demanded Lowell. "That's *me*. What the hell? Give it again." He shook the radio and held it to his ear.

Poor woman, she thought, *just like me, with two—*

No, it was herself they were talking about. It was she, Kate Armstrong.

Ted. Could they have meant Ted?

They couldn't. Another woman. There was no other—

Elaine. Oh, God, the trip to Chicago with Elaine.

And then she realized that she was projecting it all. They couldn't be talking about her, way up here in Vermont.

But they were. A Long Island mother, they had said. "In the area." That was why.

She watched Lowell flip the dial, trying to get another report.

191

"They'll probably have it again," she said, her heart beating dryly in her throat.

"I have to know! What area? What are they talking about?"

"Just wait till they have it again. Now you've lost the station."

"Damn *shit*!"

He seemed to blame her. She didn't know why.

"Mommy," said Candy, "I have to go to the bathroom."

"Then go." She glanced at Lowell to see if it was all right. To see if Candy had made him angry. Any demands except his own made him angry. He was still busy with his radio, trying to find the lost station.

"I want you to go with me," Candy said.

"That's ridiculous. You know the way."

She didn't really care. She heard herself saying things, felt herself doing things, and none of it was real. She floated on a glassy, unreal surface.

"Please?"

Kate sensed a note of desperation. Maybe Candy was sick, too. As soon as they were outside, Candy pulled her away from the door.

The air was misty and mild. "It's nice," said Candy, lifting her face.

"Yes, it is, but why did I have to come with you?"

"I want to tell you something."

About Ted. She had heard the broadcast.

"Mommy, I'm scared. Can I go back there?"

"Where?"

Candy pointed to the road. "I have to get something."

What on earth could be out there?

"I don't think so. He'll be afraid someone might see you."

"That's why I'm scared."

"Candy, what's going on?"

Candy began to cry. "My paper hat. I put it there when we came in the road."

"Whatever for?"

"I wanted them to see it, but now I'm scared."

"You *should* be scared. What have you done? Do you realize that he'll see it the next time we go out?"

"Can I get it?"

"I don't know. Where is it?"

"On a tree branch."

"I don't know how to tell him."

"Can't you just say I'm going to the bathroom?"

"Oh, Candy."

"Mommy, *please*?"

He would kill her. He would kill them all. She looked into the barn and saw that he was still fussing with the radio.

"Can you do it fast? Very fast?"

"Yes." Candy was poised to run.

"And quietly? I'll see if I can stall him."

She wandered back to the car. He was listening to music and scowling. He must have found the station and was waiting for more news.

She moved closer but said nothing. She did not want to attract his attention. She thought of Ted.

It was true. He had lied to her when he said they were only traveling together. He was seeing Elaine.

He had gone off with his paramour to a nice, comfortable hotel and left his own family to this. He had put them here. It was his fault. She would never see her home again, or her mother.

She still had the children. Did he care about that?

It was all she could do to keep them alive. All of them. Did Ted care about *that*?

What was he doing now? Was Elaine sleeping in her

bed? On her very own side of the bed?

Elaine ... Tall and blond, she thought. A bit like Lowell.

As she watched him, from somewhere far off she heard the sound of running footsteps.

Chapter Twenty - Eight

Lowell flung down his radio and jumped from the car. She saw him reach for his handgun.

"Don't!" she cried. "It's Candy!"

"What the hell's going on?"

Candy ran toward them, clutching at her side and gasping for breath.

"There's some—police cars out there!"

For an instant, Kate caught Lowell's eye. Accusing. She started to shake her head.

"Upstairs," he said. "Get the kid, get my ammo."

"You can't—What are you going to do?"

"You hear me?"

He thrust things into Candy's arms. The radio. The ammunition.

She could hear them now, like a gathering storm. She had to get Darren out of the car. Upstairs. It was safer.

What's going to happen? What are we going to do?

Darren cried in bewilderment. He had been asleep. She carried him up the stairs.

Lowell crouched by the large front opening, his rifle poised.

"Lowell, you can't!"

"Stay back and keep down, you hear? Keep out of my way."

195

She pushed Darren and Candy onto the floor, away from the big door and the stairs.

I didn't. I didn't tell the cop.

It was the hat. Candy's hat.

"Mommy, I'm scared," Candy cried.

"So am I."

She could hear voices, and cars. The scrape of metal against rock. From her place on the floor, she saw nothing but sky. Blue sky and clouds. The sun was coming out.

She watched Lowell inch backward as he sighted along the rifle.

The slam of a car door. Scrambling. Shouted orders. Then a voice blasted through a bullhorn.

"Al Torrey, we have this place surrounded. Both of you, throw down your weapons and come out with your hands over your heads."

He would never make it.

She stopped trying to think. If she made her mind blank, it wouldn't happen.

Candy asked, "Are they going to hurt Lowell?"

"I don't know."

The voice came again.

"Both of you, throw down your weapons and come out. We have you surrounded. If you come out peacefully, you won't get hurt."

His hands tightened on the rifle. She pushed Candy back and crawled toward him across the floor.

"Please, Lowell, don't let them hurt you."

Something seemed to ripple through him, but he kept his eyes on the scene below.

"I didn't tell them," she said. "I swear. I don't know how they found you."

It was Candy.

"Please? You'll go to prison for a while. It's better than being dead."

Impatiently he waved his arm, ordering her back.

"Dead is forever, Lowell."

The bullhorn said, "You haven't got a chance. Come out with your hands up and nobody will get hurt."

He lowered the barrel like a pointed finger, following. She watched him take aim. She didn't believe it, until the explosion.

The sound tore through her. Candy screamed.

"Lowell, *no!*"

He fired again, drowning out the bullhorn. They answered with two shots from below.

It's starting. Oh, Lord, it's starting.

Again she eased herself forward, hugging the floor.

"Don't hurt him!" she cried.

More shots. A shower of dust fell between Lowell and herself. She looked up to see where it had hit.

"Stop it!" she screamed. "Don't shoot!"

The sound of Lowell's rifle blocked her ears. Wood splintered behind him and over his head. She lay on the floor and wept.

They thought there were two men. If she could get his handgun, she could help. . . .

He fired repeatedly. Through his shots and theirs, she heard her children.

"Mommy! Mommy!"

Another volley. She thought, *What if they come into the barn and shoot from below? What if they come up the stairs?*

She barely realized that she was screaming, "Get the children out of here!"

The firing stopped.

The voice on the bullhorn said, "Listen, you two, if you want to shoot it out, that's your problem, but let the woman and the children go. Do you hear? Send them out before somebody gets hurt."

197

He paused to reload.

"Please," she begged him. "If you let them go, I'll stay with you forever."

God in heaven, what have I done?

But she had to save the children.

The voice called, "Al, I'm going to count ten. You'd better have those people out of there, or we'll throw in tear gas."

Lowell snorted. "Tear gas!"

She didn't think it would do any good. The barn was too open.

"Please? Let them be safe."

He glanced at her. His eyes seemed alive with a strange excitement, but his face was drawn.

He couldn't hold them off forever. She and the children were all he had.

"I'll stay with you," she promised again.

He looked back at the men below. Then at her. And the children. He didn't care about the children.

She said, "I'm not really pregnant." And, to protect herself: "I thought I was, but I'm not."

He jerked his head.

"Hey, you. Little girl. Go on out there. Put your hands up."

Candy turned to her mother in dismay.

"Thank you," Kate whispered. "You can do it," she told the girl. "Go like this." She clasped her own hands on top of her head. "Lowell, can you tell them she's coming?"

He scowled and said nothing. She called, "Hold everything. There's a child coming out."

She watched him to see if he really meant it. He was looking at the men and not at her. She waved Candy toward the stairs. Candy stood up and put her hands on her head. She looked down the stairs and hesitated.

"I want you to come, too. And Darren."

198

"It's all right," said Kate. "You'll be going home to Daddy. Now go."

Candy pleaded, her lips trembling. Then she started down the stairs and was soon out of sight.

Kate felt herself fold over inside. Felt the life drain out of her. It might be the last time she would ever see her child. The very last time.

But she had promised.

A cheer went up from some of the men.

Then they heard the bullhorn.

"That was a good thing to do, fellas. That's a good start. Now maybe we can—"

Lowell raised his rifle and fired, drowning out the voice.

He looked very alone, very young, crouched against the wall with his gun. He had been a little boy once, like hers. An innocent boy.

"What about Darren?" she asked.

His lips drew back. He muttered something. Then he jerked his head again.

Darren scuttled across the floor and threw himself at his mother, clinging to her. She held him tightly.

She hadn't given Candy a last hug. Hadn't said good-bye. She fought back tears, for Darren's sake.

"Go on, baby. Down the stairs, just the way Candy did it. Then you can go home with Candy. You can see Daddy. Wouldn't you like that?"

"I want to stay with you."

"I'll see you later." She had to say it. "Go on now. They're waiting for you."

She eased him over to the top of the steps.

"Get away from there," said Lowell.

"I—Darren—go on, baby. You can do it."

"No."

"Go *on*." Oh, please, don't make me have to fight with him now.

Darren began to cry.

"Oh, honey—it's all right. They'll take you home to Daddy. You'll be *home*."

Lowell said, "Get the hell away from those stairs." He aimed the gun at her. At Darren.

She gave Darren a gentle push. "Go on, sweetheart. Mommy wants you to go. Candy will take care of you, she's waiting out there."

His whimper was hoarse and tinny. It wrenched her heart.

"Go!"

He started down the first step, and looked back at her. "Put your hands on your head."

He cried louder, and went down another step. Her *baby*. She forced a smile to encourage him. He disappeared from sight.

Gone. They were both gone. She wanted to die.

Outside, the men cheered again. The bullhorn said, "That's great, fellas. You're doing great. Now let the mother come out, and we'll be in business."

Lowell fired. Again and again, emptying his gun. He reloaded quickly and poured bullets down on them. He was rigid, electrified, caught in a storm of fury. He would kill them all. Kill Candy and Darren. She held her breath and waited. How many did it hold? It must have been dozens.

He paused to insert another clip. The voice said, "We can wait you out, Al Torrey. We have all the time, the men, the ammo—"

Kate raised her head from the floor. "You can't keep this up forever. What are you going to do?"

He aimed and fired again. She heard it strike metal.

He couldn't really hit them. He only rained down enough bullets so they couldn't cross his line of fire.

He lowered the rifle.

"I'm getting out of here," he said.

"How?"

Still firing, he moved away from the opening, along the wall. He moved toward the stairwell.

"They'll kill you!" she cried.

"Shut up."

Running and crouching, he reached the stairs.

"Lowell, you can't!"

His eyes swept over her. He couldn't think of going out there to be gunned down.

"Oh, please," she begged. "Give yourself a chance."

His hand crept toward hers. He needed her. He wanted to surrender, but he needed her to go with him.

Something rose inside her and began to weep. It was a joyful feeling, that she could do something. That she was important. She reached out to meet his hand.

Seizing her wrist, he swung her around in front of him. His left arm clamped her waist.

It was the hand with the rifle. She felt its muzzle against her chin. His right arm whipped out the handgun and aimed it at her head.

"Hold it, coppers," he shouted. "I'm coming out and I'm bringing her with me. You better hold your fire or she'll get it."

Chapter Twenty · Nine

A shield. He was using her as a shield. To save himself.

He pushed her forward.

She staggered and caught her balance. A phantom bullet seared through her brain. Her throat. She shrank. Her being fled into a tight ball. Only her legs worked.

They were moving down the stairs. Her lips tried to form his name. She couldn't speak.

It didn't matter. He cared nothing for her.

Down the stairs.

She could see them out there in the sunshine. She saw the cars. The glint of a rifle. A uniform.

She saw a face. A face . . .

She felt the vibration of Lowell's voice.

"We're going to get in the car here. You coppers stay back or I'll blow her head off, you hear? I see any roadblocks, any cop cars, any cops, and I'll blow her head off, understand? Do you understand, pigs?"

The bullhorn bellowed, "Give it up, mister, you won't get far."

"I told you, no roadblocks. Nothing. I'm going to have this gun on her. I'll blow her brains out."

He would. He would do it.

He walked her around to the passenger side.

It was her car. Hers. It was part of her. Part of home.
She would never see her children again.

He opened the door and pushed her inside. He tossed the key. It landed on the seat. Then he slid in beside her and closed the door.

She was dead. She could refuse, and he would kill her. Dead.

She put the key into its slot.

He opened his window. "Move that car, you hear?"

She turned on the engine. Outside, in the sunlight, a car drove across the clearing, out of the way.

A car. From home.

He closed his window. They would have to shoot through the glass.

She saw someone running. Heard shouts.

No, she thought. *Leave us alone.*

Again she felt the burning in her head.

It should be quick. No time to feel it. *Please.*

Carefully, along the dirt drive. Watch for holes. For rocks. If the car bogged down, he would kill her.

"Move it, will you?"

Her children were safe.

She had promised. Bought their safety with a promise. But she had wanted to help him, too.

Stupid. She had been stupid. What did he care?

She had had chances. She could have fled down the stairs while he was shooting.

"Where—"

"Go right."

She turned right. It was the way they had come, that first time.

"You're going to kill me, aren't you?" she said.

"Shut up."

"I was honest. I stayed with you."

He pointed the gun. "I said shut up."

"Go ahead." She increased her speed. "Go ahead and see what happens."

He wouldn't care. He was dead anyway. So was she.

No, he thought he could get away. Using her.

Then he would kill her and steal another car. Another person.

Not me, she thought. *Not me*.

She swerved, meaning to turn. Go back.

"Keep moving!"

A car, back there. It was following.

A car from home.

She *had* seen the face. It couldn't be. She couldn't believe it.

She looked again.

He was following. Right behind her. He wouldn't let her go.

Ahead, in the distance, she saw something red. It grew, formed itself into a truck. A heavy truck. It sped past her, stirring up wind.

A truck. If she could cut across in front—

It would kill her, too.

He looked back. He had seen the car.

Think. Do something.

She couldn't think. The gun was pointed at her head.

"You were going to kill my kids," she said. "I don't care what you do to me."

She didn't care. It was the only way.

"Step it up, baby."

"That's ridiculous. We'll get arrested for speeding."

She rounded a bend. In the mirror, trailing Ted's, was a second car.

The police.

"They're right behind us," she said.

He looked back. "You better move it."

"I can't. I can't go faster."

Ted was closing in.

Lowell opened his window and leaned out, aiming the rifle.

Not the rifle. Not at Ted! No!

Ahead, on her right, was a grove of sumac trees.

She closed her eyes and spun the wheel.

Chapter Thirty

All around her, there were people. This time they saw her. They helped her from the car. If she could only . . .

She looked for Lowell. He would be reaching into his pocket. Reaching for the handgun. Only she would know. She would have to keep quiet.

"Where is he?" she asked, bewildered.

"I'm right here, angel." Ted wrapped his arms around her. "Just take it easy. They're bringing an ambulance. God, your face is all bruised."

"How did you get here?"

She thought for a moment that it was nice of Lowell to let her see Ted and talk with him. And then she realized that she was probably free.

Am I free? she wondered. *Where is he?*

She asked again, "How did you get here?"

"It's a long story," said Ted. "I drove all night. And you're here, you're alive. It's a miracle!"

"But where is he?"

She looked through the crowd of people. It was not such a big crowd after all. Troopers, mostly. And a russet-haired woman who was busy writing something, and a tall young man with a camera dangling from his neck.

The young man picked up the camera and aimed it at her. She cowered, thinking it was a gun.

Then she tried to hide her face. "No. I look like hell."
His flashbulb blazed, and she flinched again.

Ted asked, "Why do you want to know where he is?
They're digging him out of your car, and he's under arrest, is where he is. That's where he belongs."

One of the troopers squatted beside them.

"Mister, you'll have to be patient for a while. It happens with people who are taken hostage. They call it the
Stockholm Syndrome."

"Ah," said the russet-haired woman, writing faster.

"Who's that?" asked Kate.

"Reporter," said Ted.

"Saltport *Herald*," said the woman.

"*Saltport?*"

"They came all the way here—"

The woman flipped a page of her notebook. "This
Stockholm Syndrome . . . Mrs. Armstrong, back there in
the barn you were yelling, 'Don't hurt him.' "

"That's it," agreed the trooper. "Named for a hostage
situation in a Swedish bank a few years ago. People start
to identify with their captors."

"How can they?" asked Ted.

"It's psychological. Almost always happens. They're
isolated. They're dependent on the person who's got
them prisoner. They're scared for their lives. You have to
understand. He could kill them, but he doesn't. It's a
twisted kind of gratitude."

"That's not true," said Kate. "He was going to kill the
children. He tried—" He had taken Darren up to the hole
in the floor. "It's just because—because we've been
through so much together." How could she explain? "I
know him now. But I hate him."

"It's okay." Ted patted her arm. "Everything's all
right."

And she blurted what she hadn't meant to say. "What
about Elaine?"

"What? What do you mean?"

"Elaine. It was on the radio. They wanted to question you."

"What radio?" He appeared confused, but his face had turned a betraying red.

"They said it was a Long Island news report, that you were seeing another woman."

"That I—" Ted sputtered.

The young man with the camera turned around and took a picture of his companion.

"You can blame my friend here," he said. "She started that story. You see what a witch you are?"

"Do you mean it's not true?" Kate felt her head begin to swim. Would she have tried to save Lowell if she had known?

Yes, because of the time they had spent together.

But then she had tried to kill him. She couldn't understand.

Ted's face was still red. "Not any of it," he insisted.

"That's all right, we'll talk about it later. I want to see my children. Where are they?"

She had thought she would never see them again.

How could she? How could she even think of going with Lowell?

"They're back there, at that place where we found you. That barn."

"Yes. The barn." That . . . place.

She tried to get up, to reach her car. It was lying on its side.

"I want them. I want my children."

"This way, Kate." He led her toward his own car. "We'll get yours later. I think it may need some repairs."

"If it hadn't been for my car . . ."

"If it hadn't been for a lot of things." He helped her in, then climbed in from the other side.

"I've been thinking about a lot of things," he went on, "while I was running around trying to find you."

"Running around trying to find me?" It sounded as though she had merely stayed out a little late, gabbing with a friend. "Ted, I was barely hanging on, trying to keep him from killing the children. And me."

"I realize that. You don't know how scared I was. And when they finally figured out what must have happened, I went out of my head. I just jumped in the car—"

"You did, didn't you?"

"That's what I was trying to say. I know I haven't been the most sensitive person, and a lot of times you probably thought I didn't care."

"I suppose I can be too sensitive," she said. "But I do like to know that you care."

"I care! Oh, God, Kate, I care."

He held her for one moment, so she would know, and then they started back to find their children.